PRETTY GURLS LOVE SAVAGES 2

FATIMA MUNROE

2

Deo

Even though they were twins, even though they didn't really fuck with each other like that, Jordynn was an emotional wreck seeing her sister leave this earth in front of her, and it wasn't nothing she could do to stop it. With her twin's death, I knew she felt like she was left in the world by herself, and that fucked with me probably as much as it did her. I needed her to understand I was her family. She still had me. Maybe not Zane and probably half of Christophé, but Jordynn had me for the long haul.

The last person I cared about that died was my mother, so naturally, I went into protective mode when it came to what was mine. After I took her home, I gave her a bath and made sure she was good before I went back to the hospital to make arrangements for Journee's funeral.

'bout to make me kill some fucking body. Grabbing my phone from my pocket, I hit talk on Zane's number. "Deo."

"Where Kim at?"

"In a basement on 104th. Why?"

"Text me the address," I growled before I hung up. This whole day had her name written all over it. I knew it was a calm before the storm, but I wasn't ready for Hurricane Kim. *That's a'ight. She seemed to have forgotten who the fuck I am,* I mumbled to myself, changing into all black before I headed back out in the streets. This bitch was begging for my attention, so I was about to give it to her.

3
———

Kim

My mama cooked a big dinner of meatloaf, fried chicken, spinach and cheese stuffed shells, mashed potatoes, green beans, candied yams, Hawaiian rolls, and a peach cobbler with homemade lemonade. I got two plates of everything before I went in my room to lie down for a while. Since I didn't catch Deo earlier, I was trying to hopefully run into him tonight while he was on the block.

I'd just tucked my head into my pillow and dozed off when my mama knocked on my door. "Kimberly. Somebody at the door for you."

"Who is it, Mama?" I tried to squint the sleep out of my eyes, rubbing my blinking a few times so I could see.

"Kim, I done told you before, I ain't yo' damn butler. Come find out!"

Blinking my surroundings clear, I rolled my eyes all the way to the ceiling before focusing back on the door. I took a deep breath in before I threw the covers off of my body and stood up to stretch while exhaling. I couldn't wait until Deo—until I got out of this house. I had to get out of this house first.

I still had sleep in my eyes, rubbing my lids as my feet padded through the dark front room. I almost tripped over the table in the middle of the floor. Mama called herself changing the living room around for the fifth time this month, and that shit was still ugly. Feng Shui my ass. What she really needed was a better set of eyes to see how trifling her house really was. *Whew, chile...* I mused to myself.

Shuffling from my bedroom to the front door, I pulled it open and saw nothing but a dark shadow on the porch. My hand instinctively ran along the wall next to the door to turn on the porch light that I gave up on once I realized the bulb was blown. "Who is that?"

"Kim."

"Yeah?"

The figure reached out and pulled me out the house by my neck, covering my nose and mouth with a cloth as I opened my mouth... to... screeeeeeeeeeammmmm...

"Zane? Is that—"

Smack!

My head snapped hard to my right side with my hair slapping me in my eyes. Face stinging with pins and needles, I sat in the dimly lit room confused. Sweat seeped out of my pores as I was trying to wiggle my hands free from the cords wrapped around my wrists.

"Aye, go tell the boss this bitch woke." A dark shadow spoke sardonically as his body lumbered through the door. "She smell good too. If he letting us fuck, I'm first."

I heard a group of men laughing just outside the door, but none of them sounded even remotely familiar. *Who is their boss?* I wondered. *And why did he need to kidnap me?*

"My first mind said for me to kill yo' spiteful ass." Deo's voice came through the door. His heavy footfalls moved adroitly to where I sat in shock. "Giving a crackhead battery acid because you thought that was my wife was a bitch move. That's how I knew it was you. Sending the wife that message though?" I saw his head nod up and down against the dull light streaming in from outside of the room as he began clapping slowly. "Bravo, Kim. Bravo. Bet you didn't bank on that jealous shit getting your throat slit, did you?"

"Deo, I-I swear I don't know what you're talking about!" I lied. Now that battery acid… that was all me. I didn't send any messages.

"I see your selective memory has kicked in, so allow me the opportunity to refresh you on a few things." Pulling up a chair on my right side, he sat so close to me I could smell the Versace soap coming from his neck. "Last time we talked, you called yourself taking me down memory lane. Let's go back, shall we?"

"Deo—"

"Remember your little friend, Maritza? The one you grew up with that you told you lived with me? Remember she called herself breaking in my trap house, and you covered for her?" He spoke in my ear as tears rolled down my face.

"Maritza was my best friend, Deo. My best friend in the whole world, she genuinely loved me for—"

"She genuinely loved you for fucking with me so she could smoke for free." He interrupted. "Remember? I still got her on camera with one hand on Kevin's dick and the other hand grabbing an ounce of coke off the table. Remember? The bitch had been stealing from me for two months before your stupid ass even mentioned she was fucking with one of my people. Your best friend, Maritza."

"Deo, you didn't have to—"

"What have I always told you, Kim? What was my number-one rule when people started fucking with my livelihood? Surely you remember that." He grabbed a handful of my hair, snapping my head back as he growled in my ear.

"Bitches bleed just like us," I mumbled low enough for us to hear.

"Come on now, baby. I know you louder than that. Amp your voice up!" He encouraged me while tightening his grip on my hair and pulling a knife out of his pocket. Dragging the serrated edges across the skin on my throat, he pulled my head back so far I thought my neck would snap.

"Bitches bleed just like us, Deo!"

"Bitches bleed just like us," he repeated with a sinister chuckle. "In Maritza's case, she just—hmm... exploded. All over the place." He taunted me with the memories of finding her dead body rotting in the living room of her apartment. "That battery acid is a muthafucka, ain't it?"

"Deo, I swear, I didn't—"

"See if you knew what you was doing, you'd know a crackhead samples the dope first before they shoot it. They not just gonna jump out the gate with new product from somebody they don't know. Even fiends like that top-quality shit, wanna make sure that high gonna take them to the moon and not across the street." He put me up on game while scraping the blade back and forth across my neck. "Had you mixed it with a little something, it might've done exactly what you wanted it to do just like that." The snapping of his fingers so close to my ear made me jump slightly. "Oh yeah, I dropped that little baggie I found on the floor off at the lab so they could run fingerprint testing to see exactly who all touched it. Now I'm sure I'll find a couple of sets of fingerprints, but what if—" He rested the point of the knife against the base of my neck and began applying pressure. "What if one of those fingerprints belongs to my little Kim?"

"Deo, it-it was an accident! I-I thought—"

"Wife is an identical twin." He revealed. "You thought I was fucking a crackhead, didn't you?"

"Deo—"

"You always was a dumb lil' bitch," he spat through gritted teeth. "Always trying to be a dope girl, always trying to keep up with the Stavros boys. Always thinking you could do shit behind my back that I wouldn't find out about. Bitch, you hustling backward. If I wanted a hood bitch, I'd have one. I already knocked down half ya friends. What make you think I wanted you, Kim?"

My blood was boiling.; I hadn't heard one word he said because the more I thought about it, the more I realized the only reason I was in this basement was because his precious Jordynn was upset. "Deo, you married her? You married her, Deo!" I yelled out, unable to control my emotions. He kept referring to this woman as his "wife". We'd been in the same house for almost five years, and half the time, I was sleeping in the guest bedroom, but she comes along, and now he ready to settle down? I got the D a few months ago in his front room. He couldn't have been *that* much in love.

"To be somebody with a whole knife to their throat, you asking the wrong questions." He spoke quietly, twisting the knife harder into my skin. I felt a warm trickle of blood winding down my chest. "But because I'm feeling generous, I'll answer your question. Not yet, but it's coming. Speaking of which, bitch, you pregnant?"

"Pregnant? Why would you ask me that?"

"So you still pretending like you ain't send that Facebook message, huh?"

"Deo, I swear—"

"You just swore you didn't give Journee that baggie of battery acid either. Your word ain't worth shit no more."

"Deo, please! Yes, I was mad at Journee, Jordynn, whatever her name is—"

Smack!

"You know her name! Don't start that shit!"

"Jordynn! I was mad at Jordynn! But I promise you, Deo, I didn't send her a message on nothing!"

Deo wiped his finger across the blood seeping from the puncture wound in my neck, pressing the digit forcefully to my lips. "Bitches bleed just like us, Kim."

I parted my lips slightly, tasting my own blood as he shoved it in my mouth. "Next time you gotta piss, call X. We'll see if yo' lil' stupid ass pregnant or not. I'll tell you this though; if you are, I hope you made peace with whoever your god is. You'll be meeting him soon enough."

"You'll kill your own baby, Deo?"

"My baby?" He fumed, mushing my head. "Bitch, that could be my baby, my nephew, Steven's kid—"

Steven? How did he know about Steven? "Steven? I don't know anybody named Steven."

"Oh, now you don't know the person who got your debut video took down off of Pornhub?"

"Wait—that wasn't you who got the video removed?"

Deo's intense stare cut right through me. Even if the light prevented me from seeing his piercing, brown eyes, I felt it. "We're done, Kim. You hear me? We done. I catch you contacting my wife again, this conversation won't be as friendly."

I took a deep breath in and released it slowly, relieved. Knowing Deo's temper, I was surprised I was still alive. After all, he did murder my best friend with a baggie of battery acid that he told her was heroin. "Thank you, Deo. Thank you so—AAAHHH!" I screamed as he slammed the knife point down on my hand. The blade pierced my skin. The palm of my hand ripped open as he pinned me to the arm of the chair. My hand swelled up quickly. I felt the steel smash through the bones in my hand and rearrange my veins as blood poured from the open wound.

"Bitches bleed just like us, Kim. Don't forget that," he remarked darkly before he stood up, dusting off his pants. "X! Catch this bitch's piss next time she go, if she piss in this chair, slit her fucking throat!"

"No prob, boss!" I heard X's response, hoping to wiggle the knife from my bound wrist, trying to remove it from my palm.

"I love an efficient nigga," Deo mumbled, more to himself than me while I watched him walk calmly out the room. Dizzy from the intense pain shooting through my hand, my head began to pound slowly. Dark and fuzzy figures swam back and forth in front of my peripheral vision until I eventually passed out.

4

Zane

Me and my brother still had to have that conversation about what I did, but I gave him his space. He needed to be there to console my baby mama through the loss of her sister. In the meantime, I sent X and a couple other goons from the block to Kim's house so she could have a "chat" with the love of her life. Deo was gonna either kill that girl or make her wish she was dead.

I stepped into Deo's side of the business since he was otherwise occupied. Chris texted me a while ago, telling me to call first before I came over because he had company. Now that was more intriguing than anything; Chris didn't have company. We knew he did his thing out here, but he didn't have women running in and out of his house like we did. I take that back, like I did. Deo been wifed up for a minute; even if he wasn't claiming Kim. He still didn't bring people to his crib like that. Everybody knew where the trap house was though.

"Aye," I answered my phone from the Bluetooth button on my steering wheel. "What's up with ya people?"

"Zane Stavros." Steven greeted me cheerily through the car's speakers. "I was just about to ask you the same thing."

"What he say?"

"Zane, you know Deo already knows about our little partnership, right? Just introduce him to David so we can go back to making this money."

Steven was always fucking some shit up. If Deo knew about Boonie... "Which one?"

"The one between you and our little friend with the diamonds."

"Deo don't know about David."

"We've had a conversation recently about you and David. Deo knows."

"You talked to my brother about—"

"Listen, Zane. This isn't about you, your brother, or none of that other shit. This is about making a shitload of money for the rest of our lives. Regardless of where it comes from, all money spends whether you selling dope, diamonds, pussy, tonsils, or letting somebody tap that booty hole. Now, I don't know about you, but I'll sell my wife's snatch to the highest bidder and ask her if she had fun as long as I got paid. I've made nice with David. All you have to do is show up to Potawatomie with Deo, and we can go back to making this money. Are you in or out?"

I hadn't put any money in the family account since David walked away from me that afternoon at the same hotel this meeting was supposed to be happening at. Deo hadn't said anything, but I knew it was only a matter of time before he started asking questions, especially since Xander was one of his go-to men in the streets. He had to know Tandra wasn't doing the IG thing anymore with her doctor putting her on bed rest until she had the baby. I could do it myself. I just didn't have the patience to be in the house all day on the internet like that.

"I'm in." I spoke, seeing Deo's number come through on the other line. "Text me the addy. We'll be there." I clicked over and braced myself for whatever he had to say. Not only did Deo know about the partnership, I didn't know how long he knew. With Journee dead and Kim tied up in a basement, ain't no telling what kind of mood he was in. "Deo."

"What we gotta talk about, Zane Stavros?"

"Who said—"

"Chris told me to call you." He interrupted me mid-sentence, which meant he was on a thousand. "Meet me."

"Where?"

"How about... let's see... Potawatomie in about an hour. You free?"

"Yeah, I'm free," I responded, confused. Deo didn't gamble. "We hitting the tables?"

"Meet me at the bar."

"I'll be there—Deo?" I looked over at the console, which told me he'd hung up. Shaking my head, I knew I had to get my mind in the game when Steven's text flashed on the screen. We were supposed to be meeting up with David at Potawatomie in an hour. "This nigga..." I mumbled to myself, starting up the Jag before peeling off down the street.

STEVEN AND DAVID were sitting at the table laughing when I walked in. The smoke from their expensive cigars curling diaphanously around their empty shot glasses. Deo sat at the bar with a brooding look, his eyes darting back and forth from the men to the door and back again. Adjusting the lapel on my suit, I headed in my brother's direction as Steven showed David something on his phone. "Deo."

"I'ma ask you one more time before I go over here to this table and fuck with these two sheisty muthafuckas. What you got to tell me, Zane Stavros?"

"So much shit been going on I just haven't had the chance—"

"Yo' ass always got something to say when it comes to Jordynn, but when I ask you a simple question, you beat around the bush like Mary fucking Poppins." He threw back his shot of brown liquor, wiping his mouth with the back of his hand. "If you kept yo' head in the game instead of in my wife's panties, you'd know yo' dumb ass made a deal with the fucking devil that I gotta get us the fuck out of!"

"Deo, who the fuck you talkin' to?"

"You don't want me to answer that right now, so I suggest you bring yo' ass over here to this table." He stood nose to nose with me, his eyes black as night. Even now as a grown man, my brother put a corner of fear in my heart when I saw that look in his eye. I'd never tell him that to his face though.

Watching him take long strides to where my business partners sat, Deo headed over to the sitting area, and I signaled Steven to follow us. Both men stood up and showed respect as my brother sat down. Taking the seat near him, I made myself comfortable in my seat as Deo sat back, showing off the handle to his .9 millimeter pistol against his black tee and jeans while staring both men in the eye. "Why am I here?" He began, sucking his teeth.

"Deo Stavros. I've heard many good things about you." David reached across the small table, extending his hand to shake. Deo stared at his hand for a second before resuming his stance.

"Yet I've heard nothing about you. If you and my brother are already concocted this scheme behind my back, why do we need to meet again?"

"You don't know who I am, do you?"

"We ain't bout to go back and forth." Deo stood up and reached for his pistol. "I don't give a fuck who you are.

Zane ain't doing no fucking business with you, him, or no damn body else unless I say so!" He pointed the gun back and forth between both men, settling on aiming the barrel at David's head as a woman sitting near us looked over and let out a blood-curdling scream. Security started heading our way, tasers drawn, as if that was supposed to scare us.

"You really gonna shoot your own father?" David scoffed vehemently, lighting his cigar for a second time and taking a long pull. I saw movement from my peripheral vision, chairs scraped across the tiled floors trying to get away from where we sat calmly.

"Nigga, you ain't shit to me. My pops been in the ground for a long time now." Deo cocked his pistol before resting the tip directly between David's eyes.

"Tamiko never told you about me, I see. Ask her how she knows Steven." He slid his eyes back and forth between my brother and the man sitting next to him looking slightly uncomfortable.

"You know what they say about speaking ill of the dead." Deo warned as his finger began to curl around the trigger. Before I could react, a security guard tackled him to the ground from behind, trying to be a hero. My brother stumbled slightly, falling to one knee when I caught the man around his neck and choked him out. "GET THE FUCK OFF ME, BITCH!"

"John, what are you doing? His wife is a resident here!" the front desk clerk screamed, running over to where we were with a cordless phone in hand. "Mr. Stavros, I'm so sorry, but for the safety of our other guests, we cannot allow you back at the hotel. We'll comp your stay—"

"My wife ain't staying in this shithole!" Deo roared, jumping to his feet once he saw me let the man go. "And you buried yourself when you put yo' muthafuckin' hands on me, rent-a-cop muthafucka!" The security guard stood gasping for air when Deo swung and punched him in the face. His body swiftly hit the ground. My brother knocked him out cold. "Zane, end this shit now! And David, you can eat a dick! Fuck away from me!" Deo thundered, his voice echoing from the walls as he took long strides toward the sliding glass doors.

"Zane, I hate that—"

"Stay the fuck away from us, bitch!" I spat, tossing a few bills on the table for the drinks before following my brother's lead. Deo was right; I made a deal with the devil over money and pussy, and now that deal was coming back to fuck with me with a vengeance. The only other person still living who knew our mother's name was Christophé. "This can't be fucking life, man. It can't."

5

Christophé

"Deo, you do realize you asking me to remember some shit that happened back when I was a kid, right? How the fuck am I supposed to know who was in that room and what they talked about?" I yelled at my brother as the makings of a headache began throbbing at the base of my skull.

"Chris, I know you blocked that day out in your head. I know. I need you to think though. It's important. Who all was in the room the day Pops died?"

I sat back in my recliner, sighing hard as I tried to remember who was there. Jordynn brought me two pain pills and a cup of water before disappearing again out of the office where I sat pondering Deo's question. "Shit's blurry, bro."

"Was Steven there?"

"Steven... Steven... you talking 'bout Sleazo Stevo?"

"That's exactly who I'm talking 'bout."

"Why would he have been at our house?"

"Chris, was he there or not?"

"Uhmm... maybe? Deo, I really don't remember. I've been blocking that day out for years now."

"A'ight, lil' bro. Do me a favor though, think on it and let me know. How's the wife doing?"

"She good, just brought me something for this headache. I might keep her around for a little while." I cackled, knowing he was pissed she left in the first place.

"Chris how you know Jordynn, man? I'm really talking myself out of coming over yo' house and killing yo' ass."

"I came over to the house one day looking for something, and she was there with the designer. Funny, because the designer thought I was you until yo' wife pulled ya' gun out on me!"

"As she should have. Why you ain't say nothing before now?"

"She asked me not to. After I convinced her to put the gun down—"

"How you do that?"

"Pulled my weapon out on her and pointed it at her temple. She wasn't 'bout that life." I snickered in my brother's ear.

"See, you almost got Jenny killed. Had I came home and saw the wife dead, knowing I left her in the house with the designer, they would be just now finding her body." Deo spoke thoughtfully.

"Yo' 'I love my wife who hate my guts' face ass. When you gonna find out 'bout that baby?"

"I think somebody low-key fucking with Jordynn head. I ain't got nobody pregnant. And if I did, the hoe ain't told me. What type of shit these women be on, man?"

"That's why you don't bring everybody to ya house, Deo. Ain't no telling—"

"Look, Pop." Deo chided, he always referred to me as his father when I started speaking facts. "Only woman ever been to my house other than thot box is Jordynn."

"Who you think it is?"

"Kim. Who else would it be?"

"I don't think Kim pregnant."

"Why not?"

"Kim bisexual."

"She what?"

"After you put her out, I saw her going into this one club downtown that's known for—"

"Kim ain't bisexual. If she was, she should've been said something. Probably would still be at the house." He laughed quietly to himself. "My girl got a girlfriend," he sang lowly.

"Aye, back to Stevo. What's going on with him and Pop?"

"I don't know. Shit ain't making sense right now. Aye, I'm 'bout to pull up so we can chop it up."

I don't know who he thought he was talking to, but I knew my brother. His woman was here, it was late, and he was still full of adrenaline from what he'd just found out at the hotel. "Jordynn sleep, Deo."

"How you know?"

"She said she was 'bout to go to bed."

"Oh, well in that case, I'll pull up on you tomorrow then."

"Tomorrow, huh?"

"Yeah."

"This betta not be you pulling in my driveway, Deo. Let that woman get some rest."

"Fuck that. I got a house she can sleep at just fine. Open the damn door." He boomed before ending the call.

My brother had the front door opened, shut, and the house armed before I got to the door to my office. By the time I realized he was inside, he was already halfway up the steps. "Deo!"

"What, Chris!"

"Second room on the left."

"A'ight."

6

Jordynn

After ten days overseas, putting my name on his house, redecorating everything, giving this asshole my heart... I check my inbox and see an anonymous message about me being somebody's step mama? Nah, I ain't built for all that. Deo had to tell me something. I just found out about my own pregnancy. Fuck I look like taking care of two babies, and one of 'em ain't mine?

All these women say it ain't the baby's fault that the man cheated... yes the hell it is. Because if it wasn't for that baby, it wouldn't be tension in the house that the main woman was trying to make a home for her and her man. Just because they got a baby together, these side chicks seemed to think that gave her a say in whether or not the man could basically have a life outside of her. I ain't the one who gonna have nobody's kid running my household, talking 'bout I can't discipline him because "his mama said so". We ain't even gonna talk about the games women played when they knew the man got somebody and pursued him anyway. Nah, I'd be done killed that hoe, no cap. Like I told Deo, fuck a baby. He better be a father to mine and mine ONLY.

I'd just dozed off from crying myself to sleep when I thought I heard a noise outside my bedroom door. Waiting to see if Christophé was on the other side, I tucked my head in and was somewhere between fully woke and half asleep when the door opened quietly and shut. He must've been looking for something—

"Say what you want... but don't say it's overrrr. Call me out my name... but don't say you over meeee..." Usher's "Say What You Want" was being serenaded softly in my ear by the man who could easily be the love of my life. "You leaving me, Jordynn?"

"Yup. Go home, Deo."

"I am home. You my home. Scoot over." He nudged me to the other side of the bed, sliding under the covers before wrapping his arms around my waist. "You smell good."

"You don't."

"What I smell like?"

"Pussy." I lied. My man smelled good. He still had his signature Versace scent, but there was something else... he smelled like alcohol... some of that good kush... anger... rage... pure adrenaline. Whatever it was had me on go.

Yeah, I was hurt, but he needed to take that hurt away in the way that only he knew how.

"You a lie. Your man don't smell like no damn pussy. Liquor, maybe. Lil' bit of that premium blueberry kush, probably. I know for a fact I don't smell like no fuckin' pussy though."

"Lemme see." I rolled over and was face-to-face with his hard chest.

"Gimme your hand." He took my hand in his and ran it along his naked thigh, wrapping my fingers around his dick. "That's all you, sexy. He don't even get hard for none of these bitches out here."

"But you pregnant though." I unwillingly snatched my hand away from his grip. Not because I wanted to, but to prove a point.

"Don't be pulling away from me. You know I'ma touchy boyfriend. I like grabbing your ass..." He squeezed my booty cheek. "...rubbing yo' thighs..." He slowly ran his hand from the top to the bottom of my thigh. "...grabbing yo' titties..." He grazed my nipples with his fingertips before gripping a handful of my mounds, "...and feeling that pussy," he mumbled with his hand traveling to my inner thigh, resting his hand between my legs with the thin material stopping him from sliding his fingers inside my gushy box. "You so fucking wet. She miss me. Mmhmm... she miss Deo, don't she," he mumbled, diving underneath the covers.

"I got people in my inbox telling me we sharing some

D, yet you think you can just lick my pussy and make it better?" I scooted away from his reach. The moonlight hit his face through the curtains once he reappeared from underneath the covers looking all fake hurt.

"Jordynn, on my life, I don't know who sent you that message. Soon as I find out who did though—"

"No, Deo. You don't understand. You're pregnant." It was my turn to grab his hand and place it on my belly. "I gotta go to the—"

"Baby, what? When?" he questioned, pulling me closer to touch his forehead to mine.

"I don't know, but if I had to guess it was probably that first time we..."

Deo gripped my face with both hands and pulled me to his lips, softly slipping his tongue between my lips. I forgot what I was mad about, wrapping my hand around his neck as I wrapped my legs around his naked body. "I love you Jordynn Stavros," he mumbled, edging my panties to the side before he slid inside my pregnant pocket. "Mmm... how you mad at me with yo' pussy this wet?"

"You make me sick, Deo," I moaned, climbing on top of him. He grabbed my hips as he snaked in and out of my wetness, gently stroking my nub while I gyrated my hips in a circle.

"You love me, Jordynn," he grunted, raising up and gripping my ass cheeks. "Stop acting like you don't."

"Oouu, shit. I hate you, Deo Stavros," I whimpered, wrapping my legs around his waist while grinding back and forth. He put one hand behind him for balance, bouncing my little self up and down, my skin smacking rhythmically on his dick. "I hate you so fucking—"

"Shut the fuck up and cum on him," he ordered. "If this yo' muthafuckin' dick, you betta cum on him right fuckin'—"

Just like every other time he had me speaking in tongues, my orgasm happily sprung forth when he called. "DEOOOOO!"

"Mmhmm... she love me. Say you love me, dammit!"

"I-I love—"

"Say it like I taught you that first night, or I'll take him back!"

"I LOVE YOU DEO MUTHAFUCKIN' STAVROS!"

"You betta fuckin' love me." He continued his relentless tapping the bottom of my pussy with the tip of his dick. "I love yo' ass. You betta not ever say you hate me. You hear me, Jordynn?"

"Mmhmm—"

"Daddy gonna have to punish yo' lil' ass again. You don't want that, do you?" He leaned forward, and I fell backward. Deo grabbed me by my ankles and pushed them to the side of my head, pinning me to the mattress.

"DEOOO—AAAHHH!"

"Stop crying and take this dick. You hurt my feelings," he moaned in my ear. "Telling me you hate me, knowing how much I love you." He slowed down his stroke, making love to my pussy. "I gave you my baby. Gotcho ass didn't I? Hold yo' muthafucking ankles!"

"That's why you make me sick—DEO!" I did as I was told, watching him balance himself on his feet before angling his dick downward and quickly slipped inside my gushy. My man gripped my waist and started banging my guts with precision like he hated me. Deo had my juice box sopping wet and still dripping like a snow cone. I felt like I was about to drown in my own juices.

"Who make you sick, Jordynn? Hmm? I make you sick? You really want me to just throw this dick deep in yo' muthafuckin' guts don't you? Tighten that pussy up! It better feel like she sucking my shit!"

Deo let me know with every pump that he was in control; the only thing I could move was my lips. I was pissed, but damn if that shit didn't feel good. I felt every last stroke, every last vein on him, every last throb as his dick matched the beat deep down in my pussy. "Mmm... no, baby... you don't make me sick."

He licked the side of my face, biting my neck as I came for the second time; my body frozen in place. Grabbing me by my chin, he stuck his tongue out and rubbed it across my lips. I flicked my tongue against his before he inhaled my face. "Marry me."

"Yes, Deo... yes... whatever you say... the answer is yes." He released his grip on me, and I promptly wrapped my arms around his neck while my legs wrapped back around his waist.

"I love you, Jordynn. I'm your family. You ain't never gonna be alone again. You got me, and we got us."

"And the baby?"

"And the baby."

"OUR baby, Deo. If anybody else is pregnant, dead that shit. WE a family."

He grabbed me by my waist, and we switched positions so I was on top. "Will do, boss lady."

I loved it when he talked that boss shit to me. Something about him calling me boss lady had me going crazy. I wrapped my hand around his neck and applied pressure while I bounced up and down on his dick. "She good to you, Deo?"

"Damn, baby, this pussy good as fuck," he moaned, trying to control his nut. "You 'bout to make me cum—"

"Cum for me—mmm... there he go," I whispered in his ear with his seed spilling inside me in spurts. "There he go. That's all me, Deo Stavros. Don't you forget it."

"Never."

Collapsing on top of his chest, I listened to his heartbeat beginning to slow down and return to normal. We were in total and complete sync with one another, and it made my heart full. I couldn't believe he asked me to marry him, and I shocked myself even more when I said yes. I loved Deo, but we still had some things to work out before I could walk down an aisle and give myself to him for the rest of my life.

"Aye, I know y'all ain't fucking in my guestroom!"

Christophé yelled through the oak door. "One of y'all better get up and wash them damn sheets!"

"Aye, fuck you, nigga!"

"Betta had brought yo' ass over here. I was about to slide if you would've waited 'til tomorrow. Nutted all on ya son's forehead too!" He shuffled away from the door, chuckling to himself.

"Slide in my girl's room, and I'ma slide you in a quick prayer to let God know you on ya way, bruh!" he yelled back. "You was gonna give my brother some pussy?" Deo questioned playfully, pulling on my hair.

"Naw." I mushed his head. "Christophé was a gentleman the entire time. Now if Zane was here—"

"I'ma beat yo' ass." He leaned in, biting my bottom lip before he took another kiss. "You know my trigger finger stay on go mode. Get yo' brother-in-law shot. That's what you do."

"Get yo' lil' baby mama killed. You saw what I did to ya old bitch." I snickered, pecking him on the tip of his nose.

"Lay on my chest again. I like that." He rested my head on his heart, absently running his fingers through my hair. "Why you keep saying you hate me?"

"If I like you... I mean, seriously see myself with you for the long term... nine times outta ten, you drive me crazy. Out of the handful of people I've been with in the past, you the only one who has the power to either make my entire day or irritate my entire soul."

"Damn, baby. That's sweet, but it's kinda fucked up."

"Why you say that?"

"You know how I feel about you?"

"Yeah. You love me."

"I more than love you, Jordynn." He ran his fingertips up and down my spine as he spoke. "I wanna make you happy. The kind of happy that when you lay in the bed next to me at night, you say to yourself, 'Wow. Who even knew this was possible?' You ever been that kind of happy, baby?"

"No." I yawned softly. Deo's deep timbre was my lullaby rocking me and our baby to sleep.

"I can't wait until we get married. I wanna cuddle with you, tickle you until you get mad, play hide-and-seek just so I can scare the shit outta you..."

"Go to sleep, Deo." I covered his mouth with my hand so he'd shut up.

"You can ignore me all you want. I'm still gonna marry you." Deo pecked my forehead before I was finally able to doze off with a smile on my face.

7

Deo

Christophé's house wasn't as comfortable as mine, but Jordynn was only here for the night, so I put up with it for the time being. Not to mention, it was convenient for me and Chris to continue our conversation from last night. I had to know what the connection was between David and my parents, and although he couldn't remember exact details from that fateful day, he was the key.

I checked my phone and saw I had a text from Xander. Tapping the screen twice to open the message, I wasn't shocked to see Kim was pregnant. The question was, who was she pregnant by? Was it mine? Or was it Zane's? I didn't want to deprive the next man of his seed, but Kim couldn't go full term with this baby either according to Jordynn.

The more fucked-up part was that I cheated on a woman I claimed to love with a woman I know for a fact I didn't. If Kim WAS pregnant by me, I knew her jealous nature all too well. She'd make it her business to come to my house whenever she felt like it to rub what we did in Jordynn's face and get her ass kicked every time. As much as I enjoyed seeing Kim's face smashed against the concrete... nah. We had to get this thing out in the open. I wasn't going to subject Jordynn to that, especially with her being pregnant with a baby I knew without a doubt belonged to me.

"Hey, you." Jordynn appeared from out of the bathroom taking care of her hygiene. "You hungry?"

"Mmhmm."

"What you want to eat, love?"

"Kinda wanna spread vanilla icing on your pussy, add sprinkles, and eat it like a cupcake." I reached out and pulled her on the bed with me. "What you eating?"

"Christophé made me some food, so I'ma eat that." She straddled my waist, sitting her plump booty in my lap while she rubbed my beard. "Lemme braid this."

"You know how to braid?"

"No."

"You good, then." I smacked her ass, scraping her panty-clad pussy back and forth across my lower half. "Lemme eat this."

"You know how?"

"Hell yeah."

"You good, then." She grinned smugly, sliding her hands down the sides of her panties to take them off. I helped her out, ripping the thin material out of my way. With one move, I sat up and hoisted her thighs on my shoulders, holding her ass cheeks in both hands for balance while I feasted on her pearl. She leaned over where my phone was, turned around slightly and snapped a pic of us in the mirror on the dresser. "Deooo—mmm, get full baby."

"Mmhmm—gimme some juice to go with my food."

"AAAHHH DEO! SHIT!" I loved making her scream, that pussy right there loved me.

"That should get you through the day." I kissed her caramel-colored, peach-shaped lower lips before pressing my lips to her belly button. "Yo' lil stomach firm. Why didn't I notice that while we was overseas?"

"Because you were more focused on my lil' pussy," she mumbled as I lowered her booty on the bed, kissing me on my lips. "I noticed it, and that's why I took the pregnancy test."

"I wish you would've told me first. I wanted to be there and wait with you." I pulled her hair back, gripping her thick strands in my fist.

"With the stress of that message, Journee, and everything else going on... I really wanted to be alone, babe."

"But you called my brother though?"

"I was mad at you. Why wouldn't I call your brother? All y'all talk so much, I figured you'd find out."

"So—you know what. We'll talk about it when we get home. Where your bag?"

"I ain't going home." She scrunched her face up at me before swinging her feet over the edge of the bed, hopping down and heading for the door.

"What you mean 'you ain't going home'?"

"Just what I said. Thanks for the dick, but we still got problems."

"We still got problems? What you mean we still got problems?" I snapped. "You said yes to my proposal, and you carrying my baby, so what problems we got?"

"Deo, if you don't know, it's not my job to tell you." She opened the door and walked out of Christophé's spare bedroom, slamming it behind her.

Jordynn said I was the one who had the power to either make her day or irritate the fuck outta her. Judging by the way she was moving, it was definitely the other way around. She had me fucked up if she thought I was going home before we worked this shit out. I'd be here for as long as it took for her to understand I wasn't leaving Christophé's without her.

8

Kim

"Bitch, I swear to God—" Boonie began, unbuttoning his pants.

"It's our secret as long as you ain't recording us," I cooed, inching closer to his massive tool. "I'm not telling him, so if he finds out—"

Boonie gripped the back of my head, forcing me to go down on him. Tears rushed to my eyes, and I almost choked until I relaxed my throat when he slipped past my gag reflex.

"Mmm... make it sloppy for me, bitch." I slurped and gagged on his thick, chocolate manhood until he erupted stickiness down my throat. Whatever Boonie wanted, I was all in as long as Deo didn't find out I wasn't pregnant.

Deo was so pressed about whether or not I was with

child, I figured it had something to do with his precious Jordynn. Boonie bandaged my hand up once he left; Deo's knife went through my hand clean and came out the other end. All because of *that* bitch. Naw, I wasn't pregnant, nor was I the one that sent that message, but I'd happily be the reason she left his ass. Even if we didn't get back together, he didn't deserve to be happy, nor did she.

"That was good. Now you only owe me twelve more of those before your debt is paid." Boonie got a lil' chick he knew to doctor the pregnancy test and switched it with the one Xander had to send to Deo, tossing mine in the trash. From what he told me, he worked with one of Deo's associates who got him the interview with Zane. He worked with Zane on some special project that was top secret, and Zane sent him to the house where I was being held. They talked all that shit about them being "The Stavros Boys", yet it was only a matter of time before Boonie slit both of their throats. Hopefully, it'd be after Deo wrote his will and included me in it. The Stavros name alone was worth millions of dollars that was tied up in stocks, investments, real estate, and cash.

"Did Deo say I could leave yet?" I questioned. After all, I was kidnapped while I was still in my pajamas, which meant I was sitting on a cold, steel chair dressed in a silk robe with a red Chantilly lace teddy underneath. I stayed ready for whatever might happen, whenever it happened, even if it was at my mama house. Her front porch was dark, almost pitch black. She'd never know if I was out there getting fucked underneath the steps.

"Naw." He shoved the red face towel in my mouth, which served as a temporary gag. "Sit tight until I give the word."

Watching his huge silhouette lumber out of the dimly lit room, I waited until he was completely out of my peripheral vision before my head dropped in shame. I didn't like what I did, but it wasn't too much else I could do. My reputation preceded me wherever I went, and no matter how hard I tried to get away from it, whenever someone said "Kim", the word "hoe" always came up. After a while, I just said fuck it and embraced it. If I was gonna be labeled as a hoe, I'd be the best lil' hoe Milwaukee had to offer.

How long was I supposed to stay here, wherever "here" was though? I had stuff to do, like go watch Deo. My mama wasn't looking for me? What time was it? I dozed off for a few minutes about an hour ago, but I needed a bath and to be back in my own bed so I could come up with a better plot. Deo really thought he was doing something. I ain't have time for that "we done" shit. "We done when I say we done," I whispered softly. "And according to me, we ain't done."

I rubbed my swollen, throbbing palm. My fingers looked like Johnsonville smoked sausages each time I tried making a fist. Low key, I needed to go to urgent care, but I wanted to see my baby daddy's face once more before I did. He needed to see the pain he inflicted on me, the mother of his "first child". Giggling to myself, I got as comfortable as I could in the chair and waited for Boonie to come untie my ankles so I could get *my* husband back, and *we* could be a family.

9

Zane

"Who pregnant?"

"Yo' girl. Kim." Deo giggled in my ear, but I didn't find that funny.

"How you know it ain't yours? She lived in the house with you!" I grunted, gripping my phone a little tighter.

Deo stopped laughing, his voice dropping a half octave. "I ain't nut in Kim."

"Me either." *Wait, did I?* That whole Pornhub thing happened a few months ago. I barely remembered what happened that night. "So what she gonna do?"

"Fuck am I supposed to know? Kim can swallow a dog's dick for all I care. She ain't my responsibility. Aye, on some real shit though, why you go do the exact opposite of what

I told you to do? You think I need to be associated with Sleazo Stevo and everything that comes with that?"

"Deo, I ain't know he had nothing to do with what me and David had going on. He introduced us and said that was it."

"That's the thing, Zane; that ain't it. You know them diamonds you buying off of him?"

"Yeah."

"Blood diamonds. Know what else he smuggling in with those diamonds?"

"What? Dope?"

"Kids, man. They kidnapping kids from other countries and bringing them out here. You being associated with him associates us with that shit."

"Kids?"

"I'm 'bout to be a father soon. I ain't trying—"

"So Kim baby is yours then, huh?" I boldly laughed in his ear.

"Jordynn baby is mine."

"Jordynn?" Now I was mad all over again. How my baby mama pregnant by my brother? "Oh, uhhh... congrats, man."

"Zane, lemme ask you something. You knew Jordynn was at Potawatomie for a few weeks, right?"

"Yeah."

"All that time she was there, did she ever—"

"Did she ever what?"

"Did she ever say anything to you about anything?"

"Why you ask me that, Deo?"

"Nothing. I'm tripping. Look, I'm at Chris's crib for a while, so if you can't get me at the house, come out here."

"We making the drops at Chris's spot now?" I tried to change the subject, but my mind was still on Deo asking me about Jordynn. She must've said something to him about me, which meant she was thinking about me as much as I was thinking about her.

"Nah, drops still go to the other house. Aye, I got a call coming in that I gotta take. I'll get up with you later, a'ight?" Deo hurriedly clicked over to the other line, and I hung up, intrigued.

Deo was always telling me to respect his relationship, but from what I could tell, his relationship was more focused on respecting me. Why else would he ask me if Jordynn let a real G hit? Not saying my brother wasn't out here knocking these women down, but deep down, Jordynn knew which one of the Stavros boys would give her that work. Oouu—and now with her being pregnant, I knew that pussy was definitely wet-wet. I had to figure out a way to get close to her so I could find out.

Chris was ringing my phone for some odd reason. I was just about to call one of my trusty standbys over so I could pretend she was the woman I really wanted to be with. "What?"

"You doing stupid shit is fucking up my end of the business, that's what."

"What is you talking about, Chris?"

"I got pedophiles calling me because they heard you was in business with Sleazo. Fix this shit, Zane. I'd hate to have to body yo' stupid ass for putting money before common fucking sense!" he spat in my ear before hanging up. My phone beeped with a text message from Chris. I opened it to see what he felt the need to say as if we hadn't just got off the phone:

Stavros #3: *FIX THIS SHIT, ZANE!*

Guess I gotta fix this shit. I sighed to myself, running my hand over my head before getting out of bed. I had to take a shower and get out here in the streets. Chris was now up to deadlifting 450lbs, knew where I lived, and had the alarm code. *How both of 'em mad at me?* I thought to myself, turning on the water in the shower stall.

Christophé

WHATEVER ZANE and Deo had going on between them was between them, but when I started getting calls from anybody looking for kids, that shit was a no go. We didn't even sell dope to kids when we were younger. I damn sure wasn't about to be doing no shit like that. Plus, I had a niece or nephew coming soon, and if a muthafucka touched a hair on his or her head, looked at them wrong, or made them cry... Deo wouldn't have to handle that because I would.

I had plans on being uncle of the year; I loved kids. Kids that weren't mine though... I could spoil the hell out of them and give 'em back. Jordynn and Deo was gonna hate me, but oh well. Knowing my brother, that kid was gonna be spoiled anyway, whether Jordynn liked it or not. I hoped it was a girl. Before Jordynn, we didn't have any females in the family after Ma, and Pop gave her everything she thought she might've wanted.

Pop was a street legend. He didn't dabble in dope or anything; he just worked hard at his job. They lived in our old neighborhood for years, so everybody knew who he was. I heard whispers that he used to smuggle in that good dope from Greece, but we were so young when he died that we weren't privy to what he had going on for real.

My aunt had a nice house on the edge of the city that she claimed her husband worked hard at Miller Brewing Company for years, and they saved their money. Bullshit! She stole that money from us when my mother died. My grandma told me the whole story before she died. Long story short, Pop put everything in his sister's name in case anything happened to him or Moms, and she kept the money for her own kids when they died. We hated her when we were younger, but now that she comes to us begging for money every couple of months, it was funny. I'd tell her to call Zane, he told her to call Deo, and Deo told her to go fuck herself. Didn't stop her from begging though.

After talking to my brother last night, bits and pieces of that day all those years ago were coming back to me. I still couldn't remember who the men were in the room, but I was starting to recall the conversation I walked in on. Pop was saying something to one of the men about respect, and someone else was in the midst of speaking up when... everything else became blurry again.

The fact that this David person knew enough about us to disrespect my mother like that by insinuating she knew Sleazo... that had me heated. I was surprised Deo didn't kill his ass, but knowing my brother, David was still alive because there were too many witnesses at the casino. My brother was known for putting in work, and it wasn't nothing nice.

They claimed I was the angry one, but nah. Deo's temper would scare the shit out of the devil himself. I'd seen him torture women without blinking an eye and shoot up blocks because one nigga might've shorted him a dollar by accident. This one time, I walked up on him gutting a man in an alley in broad daylight. He turned around with intestines on his hands talking 'bout, *what you want, Chris?* What I didn't want was to see that shit. David didn't know what he started when he alluded that he was my brother's father. Deo was the type that would creep in your window in the middle of the day, slit your throat, then show up at your funeral knowing he had your blood on his hands to admire his work.

If he needed some help with that whole David thing

though, I was all in. I don't be in the same circles as my brothers for a reason, and that's because I was the one who didn't ask questions. Anybody fucking with my family got dealt with, period. My brothers had been there for me growing up, and now it was my responsibility to be there for them as men. Deo and Zane had that whole sibling rivalry thing going on, and that was between them. More Zane than Deo, but that's usually how it goes. Rarely did it go further than that, but Zane had been on some real petty bullshit lately. I didn't know what they had going on, but knowing them, they'd get over it.

Meanwhile, I had somebody I was interested in, and we were taking it slow because she was currently with somebody. I loved her vibe though. She was cool, laid back, and low key. I needed that type of woman to calm the beast that lived in my head. My rage used to get to the point where it was unbearable. Hearing from her soothed me, and feeling her relaxed me. Yeah, she stayed with her guy, but that was coming to an end soon. Especially since she was carrying my baby. I didn't want my son coming into the world thinking another man was his father.

I went to every doctor's appointment, and hearing his heartbeat for the first time was it for me. Deo knew I was trying to get out of the business, but I never told him why. I appreciated that about my brother. He never forced me to go into detail about the moves I made. Zane, on the other hand, hadn't put nothing in the money pot in a while, yet he felt like he had an equal say on everything we invested in. Most of the time, we ignored him.

Either way, I needed both of my brothers' full attention in the event that my girl's boyfriend decided he wanted to pull up on me over her. I could handle my own, but knowing who her guy was... Deo and Zane might need to step in.

10

Jordynn

"Hey, brother-in-law." Chris paused to clear his throat, almost like I was interrupting him while he was in deep thought as I plopped down at the kitchen table. "Where my food?"

"On the stove. Plates in the cabinet and spoons in the first drawer closest to the sink."

"Wow, Chris. You ain't gonna fix my plate?" I pouted, pushing my chair back and heading toward the stove. "That's how you do the mother of your first niece or nephew?"

"Ain't nothing wrong with your hands. You can fix your own food. Deo ain't 'bout to come down here and accuse me of—" He stopped suddenly. From the look on his face, I could pretty much figure out what his next words would be.

"Accuse us of having sex?"

"I ain't never accused you of having sex with Chris. Zane, maybe, but Chris? Naw." Deo walked in the kitchen with his shirt off, chest rippling, and looking like a black Adonis. If Christophé wasn't standing at the counter making waffles, I would've hopped up on the quartz island in the middle of the chef's kitchen and spread my legs wide enough for him to finish his breakfast.

"You think I fucked your brother, Deo Constantine Stavros?" I slid a small knife from the butcher's block on the countertop and held it against his right nipple. When I saw the twinkle in his eye as a smile spread across his face, I knew he liked crazy shit like that.

"And she know ya full name, big bro? Yeah, wife her up." Chris instigated, flipping waffles out of the waffle maker.

"I didn't say you did." Deo ignored his brother, grabbing a strawberry from the bowl on the table and taking a bite as I sat on the stool in front of him fucking him with my eyes. "What I said was maybe. You don't listen, do you?" he questioned playfully, pressing the berry to my lips.

I took a huge bite, letting him lick the juice sliding down the corner of my mouth. "I do listen, ass. Keep playing with me like I won't stab the fuck outta you." I was still trying to scare him, pressing the pointed tip harder against his skin.

"Mmm... stab the fuck outta me, Jordynn." He moved closer to the knife, smiling the whole time. "When you done, I'ma stab the fuck outta you next." Deo leaned in to murmur in my ear, licking his lips before flicking his tongue across my mouth.

"You just gonna stab my brother in front of me, huh?" Chris spoke up from his spot near the sink. "After I was nice enough to let you stay at my house?"

"Jordynn ain't doing shit with that lil' knife. Won't even puncture my skin, much less a damn lung." Deo cackled crazily in my face.

"Fix my food, Deo Stavros." I slammed the knife on the counter and sat back down at the table. "I want some everything."

"You want some dick too? I gotchu once you finish this food," Deo replied nonchalantly, grabbing a plate from the cabinet.

"Nah, you can keep that lil' Vienna sausage in your pants. I'm cool with bacon, sausage, eggs, and them buttermilk biscuits." I folded my fingers on the table in front of me, dangling my feet as I waited for my plate.

"Just a big ass kid, man." Deo snickered, shaking his head while piling my plate with food. "This Vienna sausage knocked yo' ass up though, didn't it."

"Anybody can nut. It don't take that much."

"Anybody can't have your eyes rolled in the back of yo'

head while you shuddering that cum out, can they?" He leaned in, kissing me on the neck. "That takes skills, mama."

"Whatever, Deo. We starving."

"Here. Eat this while I fix you some of these waffles." Deo placed a plate full of food in front of me. I didn't care that Chris was watching me. I dug into my meal. Sinking my teeth into the fluffy biscuits first, I closed my eyes and took a deep breath to savor the flavors in my mouth as Deo wiped the butter from the corner of my lip with his finger-tip. "Look at yo' lil' hungry butt making a mess already."

"Mmm, baby, why you ain't tell me Chris can cook?" I mumbled, dropping biscuit crumbs down the front of my shirt.

"Oh, yeah, Chris is the black Bobby Flay. Not only do he have his hand in the streets, he's also trained at Lé Cordón Bleu for a year," Deo quipped, forking two Belgian waffles onto another plate for me and his baby.

"For real?"

"Hell naw. Chris used to play in the food when we was kids. Give this man some flour, sugar, milk, and an egg, and he'll give you a cake that taste fresh out the bakery. He made this frosting one time with some brown sugar, cinna-mon, and egg whites that tasted like something from one of these five star restaurants. If it wasn't for lil' bro though, we would've starved a few nights."

"Where was your mother?"

"Aye, you like crêpes?" Chris interrupted from the sink

where he'd gotten started on the dishes. They say cleanliness is next to godliness, and that description fit him to a T. "I got a recipe for strawberry-and-cream-cheese-stuffed crêpes with a berry-infused syrup drizzled on top that'll put you to sleep."

"I'll put her to sleep. We don't need your help." Deo spoke up. "Eat your food, mama." Scooping a forkful of eggs and hash browns, he held the food to my mouth and encouraged me to eat. Deo fed me both plates while I sat patiently at the table and got full.

"You spoiling that girl already." Chris dried the last dish and stuck it in the cabinet before pulling up a stool to the island. "She ain't even had that baby yet, and you over there feeding her."

"Not only is she carrying my sole heir, but she said yes. Why wouldn't I spoil her?" he responded, dabbing the corners of my mouth with a napkin. "This my baby."

As happy as I wanted to be for my pregnancy and upcoming motherhood, I couldn't, knowing what I'd left at the house. That sonogram. That sonogram would forever haunt me until I knew for sure it wasn't his. And if it was, he'd never see it. "Find out about that other baby, and then we'll talk." I pushed my chair back from the table and started toward the steps. Deo stopped me dead in my tracks, reaching out and grabbing me by my wrist.

"I told you I ain't got but one baby. Even if half of Milwaukee said I got them pregnant, I ain't gonna never give a fuck about no other kids, Jordynn. You who I want. You who I need. You who I—"

"Say it, bro!" Chris yelled out, watching our hood love story unfold in the suburbs. "Get ya girl, Deo!"

Grabbing me by my chin, he pulled my face so close to his we were sharing the same air to breathe. "You who I love. I'm at my brother's house with you because of you. If you wanna talk, we can talk. If you wanna be mad, be mad. Whatever it is, I'm here. I'm at your beck and call. I ain't leaving you here or nowhere else, so when you wanna come home, we going together. You understand me, Jordynn?"

"Yes," I whispered. What else could I say? When Deo Stavros cut into me like that, it was only one thing my mind screamed for me to do. "You uhmm... you wanna go upstairs and talk?"

"Yeah, we can talk." Deo slapped me on my ass with a devilish look in his eye, letting go of my wrist while gripping a handful my ass. I took his hand and started up the steps. "Let's have some angry conversation. I'm 'bout to talk that strawberry right back out that pussy... I mean, yeah, let's come to some sort of resolution. We can't keep going back and forth like this."

"I'm 'bout to go back and forth, up and down, side to side... wait. You right, we need to be adults about this."

"Gon' hit that shit, bro!" Chris wasn't shit. He knew what was about to go down. "Take y'all ass home after this though!"

Deo bit down hard on my booty cheek as he climbed the steps behind me, and I still felt the imprint of his teeth. Swooping me off the steps, he tossed me over his shoulder and carried me the rest of the way. "Boy, I'll go soak up the sheets on your bed if I wanted to!" I yelled out from the top of the steps. "Fuck you mean go home! I just lost my sister, and I got a step kid. Hell, I'm comfortable, dammit! You heard him, bae? He said for us to go home!" I smirked loud enough for Chris to hear as I led my man further down the hall. Dipping quickly inside the bedroom right next to my brother-in-law's, I kicked the door shut behind us while I rubbed on his hard chest.

"You must not be mad at me no more." Deo pulled me close and nuzzled his face in the crook of my neck.

"I might be willing to listen to what you have to say."

"We can be adults later. Right now, we 'bout to be some savages. Is that OK with you, pretty gurl?"

"You know I love me a savage."

He laid me down gently on the bed, slowly removing my clothes piece by piece. "Only savage you need to be loving is me. After today, I don't want you to ever doubt my love for you again. I promised you that it was me and you against the world, and that's what I meant," Deo murmured in my ear while running his fingers provocatively over my skin.

"I'm not mad at you anymore, Deo," I whispered, hissing lowly when he entered me.

"I know you ain't. You wasn't mad at me anyway. You just called yo'self putting that pretty foot of yours down."

"You belong to me, Deo. From this point on, you are MINE Deo Stavros. You hear me?" I moaned, locking my legs around his waist.

"You must not have been following the game, baby. I been yours ever since that night, and you been mine. But if you wanna play like this all you, I'm good with that." He raised my leg and tucked it in the crook of his arm before positioning me sideways so he could plunge deeper inside my pussy.

"Deo—"

"I wanna hear your heartbeat in my ear every night. I carry you here. You live right here, Jordynn." He took my hand and placed it over his chest. "I can't wait to make you my wife."

"I can't wait to be your wife, Deo." I verbalized just above a whisper. Journee popped in my head. Suddenly, I remembered I had no one to invite to my wedding and no one to share that moment with. No one to be my maid of honor and no mother to help me pick out my dress. No sister to kiss me on my head and tell me how beautiful I looked in my dress and gripe about when she'd find a husband.

"What's wrong, bae? Am I hurting you?" Deo's voice was worried in my ear. My eyes were full as the wetness slid slowly down my face.

"No, baby." I sniffed quietly. "I'm OK."

"Love, no you're not." He wiped my tears with the crook of his finger. "Baby—"

"She's gone, Deo. My sister is gone. Who do..." I wept, trying to control the flood of sadness as it washed over my soul leaving me drenched in sorrow. "Who do I share this moment in my life with?"

"Me, baby. Share it with me." Deo consoled, wiping my hair back out of my face. "We're family. You know I got you."

"I know, but—"

"Listen." He moved from on top of me to lying next to me. "I don't need you stressed out, so I took care of her arrangements. She's gonna be buried near my parents on our family plot. What else do you need for me to do, love?"

"I—baby, I don't know. I don't know how these things go. I never had to bury anyone," I confessed. "With the baby, an engagement, this thing with you... I haven't had a chance to grieve my sister," I admitted truthfully.

"Take the thing with me off your plate. We good." He tucked my hair behind my ear and spoke quietly. "I don't make empty promises. Daddy gonna take care of that whole sonogram thing for us. I need to know too."

"No you don't."

"Yes I do. If I tell you it's all about us, it's all about us. Like you said, fuck a baby." He chuckled, eyes twinkling.

"How did I get so lucky to have you?" I slid closer to him, tucking under his solid frame where I felt safe.

"Thank your brother-in-law for sending me to kidnap you that night. If Zane hadn't—"

"Zane sent you to kidnap me?" I sat up, shocked that this was the first time I was hearing this story. "For what?"

"Yeah. He never said exactly why, just wanted me to scoop you up. I found out later he was in love with you."

"How though?"

"Remember that day at the airport when I asked if you knew him?"

"I told you I didn't."

"I believe you. Ever since then, he make it a point to ask about you. Chris say every time he say something about you, he always call you Zane Junior's mother."

"Wow. You realize if he would've snatched me off the street that night, I'd probably be pregnant with his baby, and you'd be referring to me as Deo Junior's mother?" I giggled slightly, wiping my eyes.

"You already Deo Junior's mother, so..." He kissed my forehead before pulling me closer to his chest.

"Deo?"

"Jordynn."

"Thank you for making my sister's funeral arrangements. I don't know the first thing about none of that."

"I know, sweetie. You just need to rest and—" We were interrupted by a knock on the door. "What's going on, Chris?"

"Deo, we got a problem. I know you and wife in there making up, but it's important."

"Go ahead, love. I'll be OK." I encouraged, knowing how my baby was. "If you have to go—"

"I'm not leaving this house without you knowing, calm down, big girl." He kissed my head and had me blushing; I liked it when he did that.

"Chris! What's so important that I can't spend time with my wife?"

"It's Zane."

Deo took a deep breath in and shook his head, opening the door. "What this idiot got going on now?" he mumbled lowly, no doubt hoping I couldn't hear him.

"You ever heard of a nigga named Boonie?" Chris questioned seriously as he and my man started heading down the steps.

11

Deo

"Country nigga?"

"Yeah."

"Yeah, I know 'im. Zane set me up with him. He supposed to be the new connect." I took a seat in the wing-back chair near the fireplace. "Sloppy nigga that don't know how to conduct business properly in my opinion, but oh well. Why?"

"According to my sources, only thing he connecting is you with bullshit every chance he get."

"Why would he do that though?" I questioned, rubbing the new stubble on the side of my face to help me think.

"You really don't know, do you?"

"Chris, don't tell me Zane got this nigga Boonie out here fucking with me over my girl." I ran my hand down my face. It wasn't even that serious. "Plenty of pussy in Milwaukee that Zane slayed half of already, so what's so special about the one upstairs?"

"I'on know, but I know he mad as hell about you and her being together."

"Still? She pregnant! And he knows that!" I roared. "This shit gotta fuckin' stop!"

"Deo, trust me I'm witchu. I see you and her together, I agree. Zane gone—"

"Crazy, my G. Zane lost his fucking mind," I grumbled, grabbing the sides of my head. "AAARGH!"

"Deo—"

"I don't know why you and the wife keep stopping me, but I'm 'bout to go do what I should've done a couple of months ago when he dropped that pin." I took the stairs two at a time to get my shirt and my pistol. Zane might be my brother, but the only person who knew me better than him was sitting across from me.

"Deo, that's your brother!" Christophé called up the steps. "You can't—"

"I ain't. Just gonna fuck his stupid ass up real quick, that's all." I stepped out of my temporary room as Jordynn stepped out in the hallway to see what was going on.

"Deo, who you about to go fuck up?" she questioned firmly. "I know you ain't—"

"I know what I said, babe. Zane—"

"Deo."

"I'll be right back, love." I leaned in and gave her a peck on the cheek. "I promise I won't touch Zane."

"Or shoot him? Or shoot at him?"

"That's my brother. Why would I shoot him?" I sneered evilly with my eyebrow raised, hoping she didn't realize I was lying. Whatever happened to Zane was his own doing.

"I don't want you to do something that can permanently affect your relationship with your brother based off of temporary bullshit. Emotions are fleeting, but family is forever."

"I know, babe."

"Deo, I love you. Be safe and come back to us." She rubbed her barely there bump worriedly.

"I always come back, don't I?"

"I'm serious."

"I'll be back. I promise." I kissed her on her forehead. Jordynn hadn't responded to me like this before. Must've had something to do with her being pregnant coupled with her losing her sister. For the first time, I had to be considerate of my woman's feelings. She was fragile and emotional right now. As much as I wanted to be close, I also had to go make my presence felt. Kim, Boonie, Zane, and everybody else who felt the need to fuck with me over the past twenty-four hours needed to learn who I really was out here.

~

NODDING at the concierge in Zane's building, I calmly walked over and pushed the button on the elevator for the eighteenth floor. As the elevator settled quietly behind the metal doors in front of me, I took a moment to check my overall appearance, not wanting to give off the look as if I didn't belong. After I left Chris's home, I stopped off at my spot and changed clothes so I'd fit in with the residents in Zane's building. Therefore, no one would suspect anything in case something went down between me and this nigga.

The ride to Zane's floor was brief. Stepping off and heading to his condo, I nodded at an older lady and her husband who nodded at me approvingly once her husband turned his head. She had that look in her eyes that said she'd ask for me to "help" her take her teeth out so she could rape me with her mouth. *Eww.*

Tapping in my code on the keypad outside of Zane's door, I eased in quietly and shut the door behind me. Strolling calmly across the expensive rugs covering the floor, I pulled my pistol from the waistband of my tailored pants and took the safety off. "Ooouuu, Zane," a woman's voice moaned sultrily from his bedroom. "Wait... slow down... put the tip in. You know I can't take the whole thing..."

"Either fuck it or suck it, Sakina. You know how I like my pus..."

I walked in his bedroom with my pistol trained on both of them. "She gonna suck it. Ain't that what they always do, lil' bro?" I laughed disrespectfully at Sakina as she rushed to cover herself up.

"To what do I owe this pleasure?" Zane uttered calmly, folding his hands behind his head while leaning back on the pillows of his Cali king. "The great Deo Stavros blessing me with his presence! Thought you didn't come to the Mil, bro."

"Ahhh, depends on the occasion. Thought about sending somebody, but then changed my mind and decided to handle it myself," I responded nonchalantly. "Tell me about Boonie, lil' bro."

"Boonie?" Zane feigned surprised, even raised his eyebrow at me. "The new connect Boonie?"

"Deo, if you just lemme grab my clothes, I promise—" Sakina leaned over the side of the bed and tried to plead her case.

"Bitch, my brother seen pussy before, stop trying to cover up! He 'married' now." Zane air quoted, his tone laced with venom.

"Please, Deo," Sakina begged, ignoring the man whose bed she was just getting fucked in. "I promise—"

"Shoot her!" Zane yelled out, exasperated. "Can't pay these hoes to be loyal. I hate that shit!"

I muffed Sakina's head backward as my brother caught her around the neck and began choking her out. "What the fuck wrong with you, man!"

"Tired of these bitches!" Zane roared with a crazed look in his eye while Sakina clawed at his hand trying to loosen his grip. "I treat these hoes like royalty, and this is the thanks I get! She in here begging YOU for some fucking mercy! Beg me, bitch! BEG FOR YO' FUCKIN' LIFE!"

I pulled the trigger, shooting a hole in the wall behind him to snap out of his daze. "Zane, let that girl go! Damn, you been wildin' out lately! What the fuck is wrong with you!"

Zane finally snapped out of his daze and let Sakina go, dropping her to the floor coughing and taking deep breaths to try and get air back in her lungs. "Get out of here, bitch." He tossed a few twenties in her direction, watching her intently snatch her clothes from the bedroom floor.

"Stay the fuck away from me, Zane! This the last time you put hands on me, muthafucka!"

I pulled her to the side before she stormed out of the apartment. Per usual, I had to do some damage control before this wild nigga got us locked up. "Aye, get cleaned up before you go, a'ight?" I peeled a few hundreds off the knot in my pocket. "I'll send somebody to take you home in a little while, a'ight?"

"OK. Thank you, Deo. Your brother been tripping lately. You need to do something about that." She spoke lowly, sliding into her clothes before leaving without another word.

I focused my gaze back on my brother, who was sitting in his bed watching me. "Let's see, you a diamond dealer that sells blood diamonds, into human trafficking, a woman beater, and trying to get me killed because of my wife. Did I forget anything?"

"Who said I was trying to kill you, Deo? You my brother. Why would I do that?" He spoke innocently, sliding his hand under his pillow.

"Zane, don't make me shoot you." I warned, pistol aimed at his head. "I love you enough to be the one to put you out of your misery just so another nigga ain't going around bragging about it."

"I'm not miserable, Deo." Zane pulled a cigar from underneath the pillow along with a lighter. Flipping the pillows over so that I could see he didn't have anything else underneath, he stood up naked with his hands in the air and a Montecristo in his mouth.

"Stand over there by the window." I motioned with a slight movement of my hand, watching him comply. "If you ain't miserable, why is Boonie trying to kill me? As a matter of fact, why is Boonie trying to kill US?"

"Us? Kill? Deo, what you talking about?" He rested his back against the window, ass smashed against the glass while he lit up. "Yeah, I know Boonie ain't the connect. Yeah, I sent him to fuck with you. You know I wanted Jordynn, and you got her pregnant!"

"Zane, you can't be serious. You JUST had a woman in here playing suck or fuck. You still pressed over Jordynn?"

"You knew I wanted her first." Zane blew smoke from

his nose before taking a second pull. "First Kim, and now Jordynn!"

"You knocked Kim down though. I'm confused."

"Yeah, AFTER you! Everybody loves Deo! Kim loves Deo. Jordynn loves Deo... EVERYBODY FUCKIN' LOVES DEO!"

"Zane, I can't believe I'm having this conversation with a grown ass man. What's the real issue, because it ain't Jordynn? Stop lying to me. We got bigger fish to gut right now."

"No matter how much we fuck up, you always been there to fix it. When I broke that window when we was kids, you took the blame. When Christophé shot Pop in the head, you told him everything was gonna be OK. When Ma started spiraling out of control, and we went days without so much as a sandwich, you went to the corner store and stole us some powdered doughnuts. As many women out here in the streets as we tag teamed, you never gave a fuck about none of 'em. Hell all three of us hit Kim off that one night two years ago."

"Damn, you know I forgot about that?" I thought back to that night after I killed Kim's friend, Maritza. We all agreed she needed something to keep her in line. Make her not forget who she was crossing so she'd never bring her friends around us again. For some reason, she still stayed, even after that. Clout chasing is a hell of a drug.

"Now you got a girl you won't share. A baddie at that.

Now you 'in love'." He air quoted. "Now you ain't your brother's keeper. That's some bullshit, Deo!"

"Zane, if I wasn't my brother's keeper, yo' ass would be dead. You hear me? D-E-A-D. Which brings me back to this nigga Boonie—"

"I'll take care of Boonie, Deo. Thanks for telling me he was on some other shit. What about this nigga David, though?" Zane suddenly changed the subject. "Does Christophé remember anything?"

"Nah. He say it was so long ago he barely remembers." I made a mental note not to show any of my usual tells around my brother. Under normal circumstances when I was pondering a situation with a snake, I'd shift my weight slightly from one foot to another so I had a firm footing when I pulled my pistol out. I didn't like that he shushed me like I was one of these lil' niggas on the block. This wasn't about Jordynn. It couldn't be. But what was it about?

"Well, we should meet up when he does remember. Take care of David as soon as we know something, right, Deo?"

"Yeah, we can do that. Speaking of which, aye, come walk me out. I just remembered I had to go take care of this little situation at the house." I waited and let him go first. My street intuition told me not to trust my own brother, and that bothered me.

"See you at the drop-off spot later. I got something to contribute." Zane's tone changed again. He was suddenly cheerful as if he didn't try to kill that girl five minutes ago.

"A'ight see you, lil' bro." We exchanged goodbyes as he smiled brightly before closing the door. I pulled out my phone and called Christophé. "Aye, do me a favor."

"What you need, Deo?"

"First and foremost, keep this conversation between me and you. Second, pick up everything at the spot and dump it in that one place." I spoke in code. Christophé knew exactly what I meant. He needed to empty the vault at the trap mansion and deposit the money in our Cayman accounts.

"A'ight. I take it you saw Zane?"

"We'll discuss that when I get back."

"A'ight. See you in a bit." Chris hurriedly ended our call. I stopped at Zane's cars, all parked in a line in his assigned parking spot, and poked a hole in one tire on all three cars. Hopefully, the thoughts that were swirling in my mind about him weren't true. Hopefully, I was being paranoid. But I noticed that when I mentioned Boonie trying to kill both of us was when our conversation changed. Boonie wasn't supposed to be trying to kill Zane. He was supposed to kill ME.

12

Kim

Deo was taking his sweet time about calling Xander, so Boonie untied me and took me home. I was hoping I could get closer to him to see what he had planned for Deo and Zane, but he wasn't budging. "This yo' house?" he questioned when we pulled up to the house next door to ours.

"Uhmm, no. It's that one." I pointed at my house while he pulled in front of the neighbor's house and parked. "You not gonna—OK." I reached for the door handle, wrapping my robe tighter around me since half of the neighborhood was outside.

"Don't forget what you owe me. I'll be over here to collect later on today."

"Today? I'm busy today. Gimme your number—"

"I said later on today." He cut me off in the middle of my sentence. "You on my time, bitch."

"So we can't—"

"I ain't have to drop you off." Boonie switched the car from park to drive as I hopped out. I barely got my feet on the ground before he sped off down the street.

Taking a deep breath in, I exhaled and ran across the yard and up the front steps, hoping the door was unlocked so I could run upstairs to my bedroom unnoticed. Even the screen door was locked, I definitely wasn't in Brookfield no more. "MAAA!" I rang the doorbell with one hand while beating on the screen with the other. "Open the door!"

"Kim what the hell—where yo' clothes at?" She fussed, pulling the door open. "You been out fu—"

"Ma, please." I pushed past her, heading for the steps. "I had a long night."

"Long night?" she mocked me annoyingly. "I'on care about how long your night was. Tell me how long his di—"

"MAAA! That's not your business!"

"Anything that goes on in my house IS my business!" she snapped. "You live here, which means you in my house! I can ask you whatever the fuck I want!"

"I got a headache, my feet hurt, and I need a shower. Please, can we talk about this later, damn!"

"That dick hit different when that bag ain't attached to it, don't it?" She sneered cynically. Mama needed some dick of her own so she could stop worrying about whether I was or wasn't getting any. "When you get out that shower come downstairs, these breakfast dishes ain't gonna wash themselves."

"Breakfast dishes? I don't wash dishes! Plus, even if I did, I wasn't even here to get no food, so why am I washing dishes?"

"'Cause I ain't, deadbeat bitch! In my house, you gotta contribute something. These utilities and that room ain't free! You don't like it, you can go back to wherever you just came from!"

I wasn't exactly in a position to talk shit since she was my only hope. I couldn't go to any of my so-called friends' houses; not only did they have people running in and out of their apartments all day and all night, but they also had roaches. Plus, Deo claimed he'd knocked down half of them, and I didn't know which half. I wasn't about to be sitting in the next woman's house so she could talk shit about how I was sleeping on her couch, and she fucked my man.

Switching on the shower in the bathroom in the hallway, I peeled my clothes off and stepped inside the nasty bathtub to get clean. My mother wasn't exactly the cleanest person, and with me being home, I guess she felt like her maid was back. Standing under the showerhead that barely sprayed water through the caked-up soap on the sprayers, I reminisced on the shower stall at Deo's encased in glass with double rainfall heads and four jets. His huge, white, claw-foot tub with the solid gold feet was handmade and took four men to carry inside the house. Once they installed it, he took a bath every other night:

"Deo, I brought your bourbon and your cigar." I walked over to where he sat soaking with his eyes closed and meditation music softly playing on the Bluetooth speakers installed in his bathroom. "Do you need anything else?"

"Yeah, come get in the tub with me." He spoke with his eyes still closed. I placed his things on the small table next to the tub and took off my heels, stepping down into the water as gently as possible so I didn't disturb his zen space. Reaching for my arm, he pulled me closer to him, and I cuddled up to his chest, listening to his heart beat opposite of my own. "Kim, you love me?"

"Of course I do. You know that."

"Would you do anything for me?"

"Yes."

"It's this one thing I've always wanted." He began. "I think you'd be the perfect person to give it to me."

"As much as you've done for me, I'll do whatever you want, Deo. What you want from me, love?"

"Suck my dick."

"I always—" I started before he opened his eyes and shoved my head underneath the bubbles. I struggled for a second before holding my breath and doing what I was told when I felt the tip scrape back and forth on my lips. A few minutes later, I felt him salty in my mouth, and he relaxed his grip on my neck, allowing me to come up for air.

"You da best, babe." Deo sighed happily, leaning his head

*back against the rim of the tub and closed his eyes a second time.
"Go turn on the heated floors so I'm not cold when I get out this
tub, then come back and wash my back."*

*"That's all?" I thought we were going to christen the new
tub, but judging from his actions, I was wrong.*

"Yeah, that's all."

*I started splashing water in his direction so he knew I was
pissed, but that backfired when he grabbed me around my neck
and threw me out of the tub with one hand. "You see me in here
relaxing! Stop acting like a big ass kid, damn!" He huffed.*

*"I'm sorry, Deo," I mumbled from the puddle next to the tub.
After turning the heat on for the floors, I came back, washed his
back, took a shower, and went to the guestroom, hoping he'd
follow me. Before I went to sleep, I prayed he'd wake me up in
the middle of the night with kisses, carry me back to his
bedroom, and apologize to me until the sun came up. When I
woke up the next morning, still in the same spot, I remembered.
Deo didn't kiss me. He never kissed me, not even on the cheek.
Once again, my prayers went unanswered; God didn't fuck with
me like that.*

Call me what you want, I stopped caring about how
anyone other than Deo Stavros felt about me a long time
ago. I wanted him back. I was already used to how his
fucked-up mind worked, so the little things he did I didn't
pay any mind to. We'd work on that after we walked down
the aisle.

"Kimberly! That water ain't free!" my mother's voice
snapped me out of my daydream. "This ain't Brookfield.

You clean enough!" I was in the middle of rinsing off when the water suddenly turned ice cold out the faucet.

"Ma, something wrong with the water!" I yelled, tangled up in the shower curtain trying to get away from the icicles pouring from above my head.

"Something wrong with the water a'ight. You still in it!" My mother's cackles were as cold as the liquid currently turning my skin blue. "This kitchen ain't gonna clean itself!"

Ain't this 'bout a—"I'm coming now, Ma!"

I hadn't planned on being around when Boonie showed back up on my block, but if this was life, I had no other choice. I was basically his slave until I got back to where I belonged. This whole thing felt familiar... almost like the day I first met Steven...

"Aye, aye, aye, aye..." I twerked on the corner of the pool table with one leg up in the air. Me, Sheena, and Maritza were in a club in Appleton showing these white boys what they were missing when I felt hands tracing the curve of my round booty. "Aye, look, but don't touch! You don't know me like that!" I yelled, smacking his hand away.

"Don't touch? Why I can't touch?" This boy looked 'bout green as a blade of grass. Me and my girls was about to come up.

"You can touch. How much money you got?" Sheena spoke up first.

"Oh, it's like that?" He stared at my ass sideways the whole

time as he backed away with his hands in the air. "I thought first round was free."

"Ain't nothing free out here, boy. These females out here got y'all thinking pussy free." I died laughing while high-fiving Sheena.

"Well, I ain't from out here, so I wouldn't know." He licked his lips at me seductively, making me wonder how far that garbage line actually got him up here in Appleton.

"Where you from, lil' boy?" Maritza challenged.

"I'm from the Mil." Stepping back in my immediate space, I felt his hand slide up my back as his lips hovered near my ear. "Come fuck with a boss. Bet you ain't never felt no dick like this on a white boy," he murmured in my ear, pressing his thick, long manhood against my back.

"Damn, boy, you must got some Mandingo somewhere in yo' bloodline. Whatchu gonna do with all that?" I cooed seductively, running my hand down his chest.

"Like I said, youngin'." Sheena had to pull me away from his thickness because I was ready. "How much money you got?"

"What you need?" Reaching in his pocket, he pulled out a knot of bills as a small baggie of powder fell to the floor.

"Oh, that's good enough for me." Maritza snatched the drugs up, tucking the baggie in her bra. "Sheena, let that girl go!"

"Yeah, this will do." Sheena grabbed the money and let my wrist go. "Kim, gon' head and give that boy that work!"

"Did you bitches just sell me for some dope and some money?" It wasn't the first time they had. I didn't do dope, but *we'd always take the money and split it between us. Now Maritza wouldn't be broke once she got her cut.*

"Yeah," my friends replied in unison. White boy was the dumb one. I would've rode that thang for free.

"Come on, uhmm... what's your name?"

"Marcus. But you can call me Big Daddy." He took my hand and led me to the bathroom in the back of the bar.

After that, we exchanged phone numbers and hooked up a few more times before he invited me to meet his parents. Marcus claimed he felt I was the one and wanted his parents' approval before we moved to the next step. When we pulled up to the apartment building in Greendale, I thought it was a joke. His father, Steven, claimed his wife was contagious, so we had to meet at his condo.

We had a few drinks, and I suddenly felt woozy. Marcus seemed genuinely concerned. He took me to one of the bedrooms to lie down for a while. When I came to, Marcus was gone, and Steven was in the bed next to me. Of course I was scared, but he explained that his medication sometimes made him incoherent to the point that he would pass out. He completely forgot I was in the bed when he used the last bit of his strength to make it into the room and lie down. He was just as surprised as me seeing me next to him. Stroking my hair as we laid face-to-face and talked, I noticed the room begin to spin again. My body was on fire when everything became a blur. The last thing I remembered was saying yes before everything went black.

I came to again, and this time, my clothes were on the floor. Steven told me I was sweating and begged him to take my clothes off. I had no reason to think anything happened any differently than how he said it did. After all, he was Marcus's father. He was also a married man and a prominent businessman in the community. Last thing he needed was a scandal that would come if I accused him of... rape? I didn't remember anything other than taking a nap.

He admitted that Marcus had a girlfriend who lived with him, and that was the real reason I'd never been to his house. I was hurt, and Steven treated me like a father would. Deo and I had just met, and we were taking it slow. I needed advice from a male figure, and Steven gave me the words that I needed.

Somewhere along the way the lines blurred between us, I think it was the day we were at his condo watching a movie and talking about my aspirations in life. We were sitting on the couch eating popcorn and drinking, and Steven started rubbing my feet. "Kim, you're a beautiful woman. You really need someone that will take care of you, pamper you, spoil you..." he murmured, kneading my toes.

"Mmm... that feels good." I rolled my neck, allowing my head to relax on the back of the couch.

"Does Deo rub your feet for you?" he continued, moving up to my calf muscles.

"We're still learning and respecting each other's space," I admitted, feeling his lips softly peck against my kneecaps. "Steven, what are you doing?"

"Showing you how you should be treated. You're a queen. You should be treated as such, love."

"Steven, you're..." I opened my eyes and sat up, moving my

feet away from his touch, "...you're old enough to be my father!"

"But I'm not." He scooted closer to where I sat, reaching over to massage my shoulders. "Let me spoil you. I can give you this condo and so, so much more if you let me."

"Steven, wait—" I put a hand up to protest. The whole thing was just too weird.

"It'll be our little secret. I won't tell if you don't." He leaned in and planted his lips against mine. I knew he felt my lips tense against his, causing him to pull away.

"Steven, we can't."

Reaching for his flute of champagne, he took a sip, returning the glass to the table. "Kim, I'm sorry. I shouldn't have done that."

"It's OK, really." Looking at him for the first time, I realized he was just a lonely, old man who needed a listening ear. His wife was still sick, so he'd moved into the condo for a while and would go back and forth between his office in downtown Milwaukee to his home in bucolic Caledonia and back to his condo in Greenfield. At his age, I was sure the back-and-forth was tiring to say the least. Taking a sip from my glass, I leaned over and gave him a friendly peck on the cheek. "It'll be OK."

"I guess you're right." He sighed deeply, settling back on the couch. "Can't blame me for trying though."

Stealing glances in his direction, I felt sorry for him. He looked so sad and was genuinely apologetic. Marcus did hand me a wad of money that first night, and I never saw him go to work while we were together. He had to have been getting money from his father. Steven wasn't really that bad looking.

Actually, he looked damn good for his age. And he did say it would be our little secret...

"Hey." I rested my feet back in his lap, accidentally nudging his semi-hard member in the process. "Can you rub my feet again? I think I'm starting to get a cramp."

"You sure? I don't want you to think I'm pressuring you to do anything you don't want to." He resumed my massage more vigorously than before.

"I'm sure. Our little secret, right?"

"Of course. I don't kiss and tell."

"What do you do after you kiss?" I questioned, moving my feet. It was my turn to scoot closer to where he sat as we locked eyes.

"Kim, I will put two fingers in you and eat your pussy clean the fuck out right now. Don't fuck with me," he murmured huskily, spreading my legs open.

"I'm fucking with you now," I moaned, feeling his stiff fingers press against my middle. "Mmm... show me what you got."

After that night, Steven and I started seeing each other on a regular, sometimes twice a week. We didn't always have sex. Sometimes he just wanted to eat my pussy. Since Deo told me he didn't do those types of things, I figured why not. Moving in with Deo, I had the best of both worlds. What my man wasn't giving me, Steven was. Deo gave me money every now and then, and Steven made sure my pockets weren't empty every time I saw him.

At one of his infamous day parties, I was introduced to

David, who told me he was a diamond broker. Steven excused himself, leaving us for a few minutes to talk to the mayor. All I saw was dollar signs listening to David explain all the places in the world where he had clients. Seeing Steven head back in our direction, he slipped me his card in case I needed something unique for a special occasion. Instead of using that number for business, I used it for my own pleasure. David felt the connection between me and him the same as I did, so we got together whenever he was in town. He told me he knew I was with Steven and didn't want to complicate things, so I put my mouth on him, and he'd give me a couple of hundred for that.

Deo still wasn't opening up to me like I was with him, yet I still had needs. The closest that David could drop me off near my house where Deo wouldn't get suspicious was Brookfield Square Mall, so after an afternoon of pleasure, I went to H&M to see what they had. Sometimes I could find a cute dress or some pants. I bumped into Ronnie while I was looking at a cute pair of panties that he promptly snatched up in the middle of me reaching for the lace thong:

"I was looking at that."

"And?" He smacked his lips at me. "You ain't at the register, so these still belong to H&M."

"Look, you cheating muthafucka, it ain't my fault you trying to get back in the house," I growled lowly at the man standing in front of me looking like he played ball. "Shouldn't have been out here cheating in the first place if you ask me.

These panties mine though. See how pretty they'd look nestled in the split—"

"Of MY ass, bitch." He finished, matching my tone while seething in my direction. "See, that's what's wrong with you straight bitches... always think a man cheating with another bitch, when in actuality, he like dick just like you! Plus, my man loves this color on me!"

"Oh, excuse me, bitch!"

"You excused, fish!" He stormed in the direction of the cash register before stopping short. "No... no... no... why is she here?" He rushed back to the panty table.

"You still got H&M panties in yo' hand though." I stared pointedly as he quickly dropped the lace material back on the table.

"Look, fish, I know you don't know me, but can you do me a favor? Please!"

"What you not gonna do is keep calling me fish when my name is Kim."

"OK, Kim. Can you pretend to me my... my uhmm... my woman?" He made a face like the words burned on his tongue.

"Don't we like the same thing?"

"Hell yeah, bitch!" he said a little too loud. An older woman came in the store, making a beeline to where we stood still arguing over the lingerie table. "Just follow my lead."

"Ronnie, where have you been!" The woman pulled him close, kissing him on the cheek. "Mama hasn't seen you in two months!"

"Mama, you know how it is when you're planning a

wedding with the love of your life." He took my hand in his with a strained smile.

"Oh, so this must be the fiancée." She beamed in my direction. "Nice to finally meet you, daughter-in-law!"

"Uhmm... hi... Ma?"

"Ronnie, she is absolutely gorgeous! Now I see why you've been keeping her to yourself!" she continued. "Hopefully, I'll be getting some grandbabies soon!" She rubbed my stomach gently.

Not in this lifetime you won't, *I thought, returning her cheer.* "We're working on it!"

"Bring her over to the house Friday. Your father is having a fish fry, and he wants everyone there." His mother continued rambling on and on, not seeing the look on my face until I busted out laughing. "Something funny, dear?"

"Oh, I was just thinking about something Ronnie said right before you walked up." I wondered how far I could go with this conversation before this stranger told his mother the truth about his secret life. "I'd LOVE to come and meet the rest of my family!"

"Then it's settled!" She squealed, giving me a tight hug before turning to give him a kiss on the cheek. "See you soon, sweetheart! You too, daughter-in-law!"

Finally leaving, I turned to Ronnie with a smirk on my face. "Thank you." He sighed with relief. "I know I don't know you, but you didn't have to do that."

"I need at least three carats." I began, grabbing the panties he'd tossed on the table before he was interrupted.

"Excuse me?"

"*Three carats and two thousand dollars a week would be a good start.*"

"*I ain't—*"

"*Aht aht, your mama came through here dripping. I know quality when I see it. Now if you had to ask a complete and total stranger to be your fiancée, I'm guessing old Mama Rose don't know her baby boy like dick. We can keep it between us. I'll even come to the fish fry. But I need three carats and two thousand dollars.*"

"*What if I say no? You ain't never gonna see me again!*" he interjected.

"*You could, but you don't look like the type to break your poor, old mother's heart. Gimme your phone, and pay for my panties.*"

"*What you need my phone for?*"

"*I'd think that you and your fiancée would need to be in some type of communication to get the address, right?*"

"*I ain't doing two thousand a week. A thousand whenever I need you, and I don't wanna hear that shit about you busy either. These would've looked better on me anyway,*" he grumbled, snatching the underwear from my hand and walking to the register.

"*Ask your favorite uncle what they look like after I fuck him in yo' mama bathroom.*" I spoke absently from behind him.

I've lived a crazy life and done some even crazier things. But I was still willing to give all that up for my husband and the father of my fake baby. Somehow, someway, Jordynn had to go.

13

Zane

After Deo left, I finished my cigar before hopping in the shower. David had been blowing my phone up since we left him in the hotel, and I wasn't in the mood to hear nothing he had to say. This man said he was Deo's father and insinuated my mother wasn't faithful to Pops. He knew Deo was my brother... all this time, he'd been using me to get to him. I ain't like that shit.

"What you want?" I decided to see what he had to say. Wasn't like Deo was gonna be around for much longer in the first place.

"I'm not understanding what the issue is." David's English accent came through my phone thickly. "How do you not see the resemblance between me and your brother?"

Deo looked like a slightly darker version of my father. He didn't look... like... "That wasn't the time or place for you to have that conversation with him, whether you are or aren't. What did you think he was gonna do?"

"Regardless, have your brother call me so he and I can talk man-to-man. He doesn't need to be in this small town running drugs when he's the heir to—"

"To what?"

"Have your brother call me. Goodbye, Zane Stavros." David abruptly ended the call.

Heir? To what? I rubbed my beard, wondering who I could call to have a check done on David. I didn't even know where this man came from. Steven introduced us. *Steven.*

I dialed his number next. Somebody knew this man's background. He and David, at the very least, knew each other, and all I needed was a link. "This call better be an apology."

"It ain't. Where ya boy Dave come from?"

"Zane, I told you what makes my dick hard—money and pussy. That's it. All this reuniting with long-lost relatives ain't got nothing to do with me."

"You introduce me to this man as somebody who I can make a lot of money with, he tells my brother he's actually his father, and now you don't know nothing? That's foul, bruh."

"Listen. I'm a business, man. I'm losing money just in me having this conversation with you, and since all you trying to get information, this call is over." Steven was the second person that hung up in my face today.

Shit, shit, shit. David wasn't talking, Steven wasn't talking, and I knew Deo wasn't trying to hear nothing David had for him. On top of that, Boonie... shit, Boonie. Boonie was on his way to Deo's to kidnap Jordynn. She was my contribution to the family business that I wasn't giving up. Hmph, fuck Deo, David, and all that other bullshit. I was about to take what was rightfully mine in the first place.

Me: You still on track to go pick up that package?

B.: Almost there now. I'ma text you in a min.

Me: A'ight.

I couldn't wait to see the look on his face when he saw me with his girl. That'll teach his ass to stop taking what was mine just because he was the oldest. I'd even let him have that baby she pregnant with. *After all, I am my brother's keeper.*

14

Jordynn

As soon as Deo left the house, I was on edge. For some reason, I felt like something was going to happen between him and his brother, and I didn't want to be the cause of why they were going through it. Christophé did what he could to keep my mind off of what was going on, but he had his own life to worry about.

When I told him I was pregnant, he told me he had a baby on the way too. I guess it was easier explaining to me who he knocked up because I didn't know her, but Deo and Zane did. According to him, it might cause a rift in their operations, and he didn't exactly know how to handle it. I told him he had to pick a time and place because that was a conversation that needed to be had soon. No man who was a man wanted his son calling another man his father. The way his face lit up when he told me about hearing his son's heartbeat and seeing his face on the ultrasound though... I couldn't wait until our baby was in my arms.

"Chris, I'm going to the house to grab some shoes." I stared out the window in the front room rubbing my little pooch. Deo wanted to be at my first doctor's appointment, but I told him I'd be OK. In the meantime, Chris offered to come in his absence.

"Shoes? You ain't bring no shoes with you?"

"I didn't grab the ones that go with this dress," I whined.

"Aye, cut that whining shit out. I ain't Deo." Chris cut into me like I was his real sister. "If you ain't got no shoes to wear with that dress, then change."

"I look cute in this dress though."

"That dress that you ain't got no shoes to wear with, though." Chris shot back quickly. "Put on something else. I ain't going all the way over to Deo's for some shoes."

"Y'all make me sick," I grumbled, stomping up the steps. "I wanna wear this dress."

"You know, if you knew how to drive, you could take yourself."

"Deo got me an Uber account—"

"Uber my ass. You ain't giving them people my gate code." He scoffed. "You can change. Stop acting so damn spoiled!"

"I'm telling—" I stopped when Chris's phone interrupted us with a text followed by a phone call.

"Deo, can I—what? Nah, she here. Who at yo' house? Well, how he get past the gate? How you know? Damn, bro. That's fucked up. A'ight, lemme know what you trying to do."

"What happened?" I froze in a panic. Somebody was at my house... I almost went over there for some shoes. Who knew what would've happened?

"Nothing you need to be worried about. We handling it. Come on, so the doctor can tell us about this baby."

Deo wouldn't want me worried, but that didn't stop me from worrying. "Are you gonna tell me what's going on? Who was at my house?" My patience was running thin with these Stavros brothers and all these secrets. Every time I turned around, they were having hushed conversations about something like I wasn't even there.

"Ask ya man. That ain't my place. What is my place is to get you down here to this doctor's appointment and find out about my niece or nephew before my brother hit the roof."

Texting Deo three question marks, I grabbed my purse and followed his brother to the car. Bae responded with three kissy-face emojis as if he didn't just call here in a panic. I wasn't gonna do this whole thing over the phone. I knew I'd get better results from him in person anyway.

～

"So Ms. Young, there's no doubt that you're almost fourteen weeks." The Asian doctor smiled pleasantly as she wiped the gel from my stomach. "Baby's heartbeat is strong, so we know he's healthy. I'm going to prescribe prenatal vitamins for his growth and development, and we need to see you back here in two weeks for the ultrasound, four weeks for your next appointment. Any questions?"

"Just so we're clear, you only heard one heartbeat, right?"

"Yes, Ms. Young. I know you were concerned with you being a twin that you were pregnant with more than one baby. However, I only heard one heartbeat."

"First and foremost, her last name is Stavros, not Young." Deo spoke up. Chris and I walked in the doctor's office, and he was sitting in the waiting room reading the latest issue of *Parents* magazine. "Second, how do we know he's OK based off of his heartbeat? He could have three fingers or frog legs. How can you tell from his heartbeat that he's healthy?"

"Mr. Stavros, that's why we do the ultrasound," she replied calmly. "In two weeks, we'll see what baby looks like and the sex. Even if your child does have three fingers or frog legs, that doesn't mean that they won't be healthy."

"But how do you know that though?"

"First-time parent?" We nodded our heads in unison. "I see. Believe it or not, this is common for first-time parents. Trust me, Mr. Stavros, there is nothing to be worried about unless frog legs and three-fingered individuals run in your family."

"I'm not the one over here passing down Kermit traits, baby, so if our child does have that, it came from you." I tittered, pulling down my shirt.

Deo kissed me on my forehead, and I noticed a concerned look behind his eyes. "We ain't got no Kermit traits either, babe, so he should be OK."

"She didn't say the baby was a boy, love." I returned his kiss, pecking my lips against his scruffy chin. "We could very easily be having a girl."

"Come on now, Jordynn. I ain't put in all that work for you to be pregnant with a girl out the gate." Deo raised my shirt up and kissed my belly button. "You carrying Deo Constantine Stavros II, that's facts."

"I could very easily be carrying Journee Celeste Stavros too. I put in some work myself that night." I reminded him.

"How pregnant did you say we was, Doc?"

"Almost fourteen weeks, give or take—"

"What's that on a real calendar?"

"Three and a half... almost four months." She chuckled.

"Oh, yeah, that was that first night then." Deo nodded smugly. "You might've contributed, but I definitely gave you this di—"

"DEO!"

"Had you screaming just like that too, only a little louder." He put his hand out to help me off of the examining table.

"Dr. Wu don't wanna hear all that!" I punched him in his arm.

"Believe me, Mrs. Stavros, I've heard worse." She smiled, handing me my prescription. "You can have that filled, or if there's another brand you prefer, that's fine. Whatever you decide, make sure you're taking your vitamins once a day, every day in the morning with orange juice so your system absorbs it better. I'll see you guys in a month, OK?"

"OK," we replied in unison. "Stop copying me, Deo." I punched him again.

"I don't know why I didn't realize before that you two are married. It's obvious now," Dr Wu remarked, walking out of the exam room.

"Don't be embarrassing me in front of these people, Jordynn." Deo grabbed my butt before grabbing my waist, pulling me closer to him. "Got the doctor thinking I didn't lock and load this thang right here." He rubbed my belly to solidify his point.

"Whatever, Mr. Stavros. Anyway, who was at my house earlier?" I questioned as we walked out of the doctor's office together.

"Nobody."

I stopped short on the sidewalk with my hand on my hip. "So now we lying?"

"Can I finish?" He grabbed my wrist, pulling me back to his side. "Nobody you need to be worried about."

"I shouldn't be worried, huh? Well, I'm about to go home then." I watched him open my door once we got to the truck.

"No the fuck you ain't." Deo spoke, remarkably calm. "House ain't safe right now."

"See, I knew something was going on! Why you keep shutting me out?"

"Do you know what would happen if something happened to you, Jordynn? You my world. Ain't nobody safe out here if I lose you. I can't take that chance."

"And you're the air I breathe. What makes you think I want to take that kind of chance with you, Deo?" I spoke my truth. "You're my only family until this baby comes out. I want you there, not FaceTiming me from prison or Chris talking about how proud you *would've* been."

"Jordynn, nothing—"

"That's what you say, Deo, but look at the life you live—"

"I was in the life when you met me, Jordynn."

"But I didn't meet you because of the game, Deo! You said it's us against the world, right?"

"We are, so what you mean?"

"Yet I can't go home, you and Chris been whispering in corners ever since you been at his house, and now, you and Zane fell out. When does it end?"

Deo sighed as we sat at the stoplight. I could tell by his

facial expression he was choosing his words. "Zane went into a partnership with Sleazo against my advice, and now the nigga that he working with claim he my real pops."

"Wha-What? How is that possible? And who is Sleazo?"

"My father died when we was kids. Christophé shot him in the head by accident on his seventh birthday. Right now, who Sleazo is doesn't matter."

"Oh my God!"

"Yeah, so now this David person wanna meet up with me to talk." He finished once the light turned green. We rode down the street in silence. I was in complete shock at what I just heard. Chris told me stories about how close they used to be, but now, looking at them, you couldn't tell Zane and Deo were related or that Chris was carrying around the burden of killing his father.

"Are you going to talk to him?"

"No."

"Why not?"

"What I'm supposed to say? I ain't never heard of this nigga until the other day, now... man, naw. Much shit as we went through in that house after Pop died... it's too late. It's too late, man." Deo shook his head with finality.

"Baby, you should at least hear him out. Maybe he is... maybe he ain't. At the very least, get a DNA test to see if you're related, and then go from there. If he is, you need to know his family history so I'm not out here giving birth to Kermit the fucking frog for real."

Deo glanced at me sideways before he busted out laughing. "Aye, don't be talking 'bout my baby like that. 'Whether he has frog legs or not, he'll still be a healthy baby,'" he mimicked my ob-gyn.

"Shiiii... y'all can have that healthy baby, I'm out." I threw up the peace sign, shaking my head. Deo fine and all, but if he got all these tadpoles out here waiting to see the light of day I wasn't gonna be a part of it.

"Listen, baby, I'll call the man, a'ight?" Deo scrolled through his phone and hit talk. Since his Bluetooth was connected to the truck, any activity on his phone popped up on the console. I'd been forced to listen to the car read his text messages more than once. As the phone rang in the car's speakers, I glanced at the console and saw an overseas number on the screen.

"Allo? Deo?"

"Aye, meet me on the lakefront so we can have this conversation."

"Where, and what time?"

"You know where Veteran's Park is?"

"I'll find it. What time?"

"'Bout an hour. That'll give me time to drop wife off—"

"Drop me off? Oh no, hunny, I'm coming too!"

"Hold on a sec." Deo put the call on mute before turning to me. "No, big mama, you gotta go home."

"You said I can't go to my house, and I'm not going to Chris's without you."

"Jordynn—"

"Deo." I rolled my eyes in his direction before staring him in the face.

"I don't like you no mo'." He huffed, taking the phone off mute.

"I don't like you either, but you heard what I said." I folded my arms across my chest and pouted.

"Aye, wife coming too." He gave me another sideways glance, shaking his head.

"Thank you, Deo. I'd love to meet your wife."

"We bringing a DNA kit too. That's not a problem, is it?" I yelled out, watching my boo frown his face in my direction.

"No, please do. I didn't expect you to take my word for it. You're what, thirty-two now, right, Deo?"

"Look, we'll see you in an hour." Deo hit end on their call as we pulled into the CVS parking lot. "I can't do this, man."

"Why?"

"This nigga... I can't do this, man! Pop been dead for twenty years! I been taking care of my brothers for twenty years! Now this nigga come along and say those ain't my full-blooded brothers but they my half brothers instead?" he expressed, pounding on the steering wheel.

"Deo, whole or half, Zane and Chris are still your brothers! But you owe it to not only you, but to your baby to know your heritage."

"You right." My future husband sighed, running his hands down his face. "You right. This just some crazy shit.

Nobody refers to my mother as Tamiko. The fact that he knew her name, man... just the fact that he knew her name..."

"Your mom's name is Tamiko?"

"Yeah, why?"

"Oh, no reason. I'm sure it's just a coincidence."

"What's a coincidence?" Deo pressed.

"No, my mom's best friend's name was Tamiko too. That's funny, right? Two black women named Tamiko who lived in Milwaukee at the same time." I giggled nervously to myself. *She couldn't be...*

"What did you say your mother's name was?"

"Diane."

"Auntie Diane?"

"Auntie? Deo, don't tell me—"

"No, she wasn't my real auntie." Deo put his hands up, laughing. "She was my mother's best friend, used to come around from time to time. Last time I saw her was at—aw, hell naw."

"What, Deo? When was the last time you saw her?"

"Christophé's seventh birthday party."

15

Deo

For Milwaukee to be as big as it was, this really was a small town. Maybe it was time for me to leave. Finding out our parents knew one another was fucking with my head. I never knew Auntie Diane had kids, especially not two twin daughters. Never could anybody have told me back then that twenty years later, I'd be burying one of those daughters while the other one was pregnant with my first kid.

"Uhmm... let's just go see what this David person has to say for himself, and then go from there." Jordynn spoke quietly after I got back from grabbing the DNA kit.

"Yeah."

We pulled up to the park on the lakefront five minutes ahead of time, and David was already there. Putting my irritation to the side because Jordynn asked me to, I got out and opened her door first before we walked hand in hand to meet the man who claimed he was my biological father.

"Nice to meet you under more pleasant circumstances." David began. "Last time we met was a little hectic, eh?"

"Let's go over here and sit down. Wife pregnant." I spoke quietly, ushering Jordynn to a bench near the water to sit. "Talk to me, Dave." I sat next to her, stretching my arms along the back of the bench before switching my gaze to the water.

"Hmm, where should I start?"

"The beginning would be nice." Jordynn spoke snidely, which was a little out of character for her.

"Of course. Steven introduced me to your mother at a day party—"

"A day party." I shared my disparaging opinion about Milwaukee's shadiest businessman, shaking my head. "Steven and the muthafuckin' day parties. Ol' bastard don't do nothing at night?"

"Well, according to Steven, nighttime was reserved for—"

"Forget I asked. Continue, man."

"Tamiko was a very attractive woman. The minute she and Diane walked in, every man—" He stopped for a second and took a deep breath. "Every man in there wanted her. Diane too, but she wasn't interested in men."

"My mama wasn't gay!" Jordynn hopped up and charged in his direction. I snatched her up before she overexerted herself. Doc didn't put her on bed rest, but she didn't need to be agitated while she was carrying my child.

"I never said she—Deo, who is this?"

"It's complicated, man. I just found out myself about twenty minutes ago," I explained.

"Let me go, Deo!" Jordynn yelled. "Diane was my mother, and if I find out you did anything to her—" She walked up on him, pointing her finger in his face.

"No, I'm not saying she was gay. You're a lot like her as a matter of fact." David smiled, hoping to calm her down. "She just wasn't interested in any of the men at the party, that's all."

"Yeah, clean that shit up, nigga." Jordynn nodded, walking back to her spot on the bench next to me. "Hate to see your James Bond–looking ass floating in this lake, but then again, too, my man is efficient. He'll make sure you sink."

"Jordynn?"

"What?"

"Girl, sit down and chill. Let this man finish his story." I rubbed her leg to help soothe her nerves.

"Can I continue?" David questioned, snickering at tough Theresa next to me.

"Yeah, go ahead, man."

"Deo, as you know, Steven's day parties are nothing more than connecting women with men for a specific 'service'." He air quoted slyly. I knew what he meant: Sleazo was a pimp who didn't check for ID. "So me and Tamiko exchanged phone numbers, and we... 'connected' a few times. We weren't exclusive, but I was a little offended when she told me she wasn't gonna see me no more because she was getting married."

"How long had y'all been 'connecting' before she told you that?"

"Me and Tamiko saw each other whenever I was in the States, so on and off... about three years," David admitted.

"And in three years, you didn't know she was in a whole relationship?"

"Like I said, we only saw each other when I was here. We wasn't on the phone for hours at a time, we wasn't sending letters and shit every week, wasn't no 'I love yous' exchanged. No feelings involved. We was just..."

"Just what?"

"Connect buddies."

"Connect buddies?" Jordynn interrupted again. "What is a connect buddy?"

"I think he saying they were fuck buddies, baby." I saved David from getting punched in the jaw, yet I appreciated that he didn't call the situation what it actually was.

"Oooohhh, OK."

"We hooked up one more time before she got married, and then she moved and changed her number. I was back at Steven's day parties and bumped into Diane sometime later who told me she thought Tamiko's oldest son, Deo, favored me. I waved it off, but she was serious."

"Baby, now that he mentions it, you do kinda—"

"I ain't trying to hear that shit. Let's do this test so we can go our separate ways." I waved both of them off, heading back to the truck to get the DNA test that Jordynn left in the front seat. My phone was flashing with Zane's number on the screen, but I wasn't in the right frame of mind mentally to hear what he was talking about. Walking back to where they sat chatting away, I had no doubt they exchanged phone numbers to talk later. David knew about both of our mothers' secret lives. I didn't care, but Jordynn seemed genuinely curious.

"I'll open it for you." Jordynn volunteered, seeing how I sat staring at the bag with my mind somewhere else. I'd been Deo Constantine Stavros my whole life, but now there was a possibility I wasn't. I had another man's name attached to mine that I probably wasn't no kin to. Who the fuck was I then?

We did the test and sealed everything up, making sure all boxes were checked and signatures in place. "OK, now what?"

"I'll take this down to FedEx. The sooner they get it, the sooner they can process it and let us know." Jordynn spoke up. "That way, we know who's who and what's what."

"Until then, I don't think we have anything else to talk about, bruh. If you ain't, then it ain't no love lost."

"And if I am?" David questioned squarely.

"We already thirty-two years in without speaking, so let's go for thirty-two more." I turned my back to him, shoving my hands in my pockets.

"DEO! Don't say that!" Jordynn yelled from behind me.

"Fuck that nigga, man! You knew about me when I was a kid, but thirty-two years later, you decide we should have a relationship? Man... Christophé Achilles Stavros Sr. will ALWAYS be my father! That's been the man that was always there, and if it wasn't for little bro, he'd STILL be here! Fuck him!" I roared, swiftly walking back to my truck. I was heated. Jordynn knew I was pissed.

Climbing in on the driver's side, I slammed my door, watching Jordynn and David continue their conversation as he escorted her to my vehicle. *That's the least you can do,* I thought, watching as they exchanged a small hug before he opened the door for her to get in. She waved at him one last time before I started up the truck and tried to run his ass over.

"DEO! Don't hit David!" Jordynn screamed just as I swerved in the opposite direction.

"Why you so friendly and concerned about his well-being?" I growled. "He trying to 'connect' with you too?"

"Yeah, but not the way you making it seem. Deo, I know you're upset—"

"Oh, you a mind reader now?"

Jordynn stared at me for a minute before she turned around and grabbed her purse from the back seat. "You know what? You can let me out at this next corner coming up."

"Where the fuck you going?"

"I'm not in the mood for you and your fucked-up attitude, Deo! He knew my mother too!"

"Oh, yeah? Did he fuck your mother too? Was Auntie Diane one of his fuck buddies? You got a little brother or sister out here that you ain't know nothing about!"

"I don't know what they did! I wasn't there! He probably did fuck my mother! I don't know! I know it ain't nothing me or you can do about something that happened over thirty years ago, Deo! That ain't got nothing to do with us!"

"Lemme ask you this, Jordynn." I pulled over at the next corner and threw the car in park. "You so dead set on me and him getting to know each other and be friends and shit. He know your mother too. Who your pops?"

"What?"

"You heard me. You taking up for this man, and for all you know, we could be brother and sister."

Jordynn stared at me for a second with tears in her eyes before she got out of my truck, slamming the door behind her. "FUCK YOU DEO!"

"FUCK YOU, JORDYNN!" I yelled, pulling away from the curb. She didn't mind dishing it out, but when it came back around, she couldn't take it.

I got to the next corner and heard someone screaming my name. Of course I looked around first before checking the rearview mirror. A black Riviera was at the curb and still running where Jordynn was standing a minute before. Throwing my truck in reverse, I hit the gas and lurched backward. Jordynn was swinging her arms for a second before some nigga reached up and punched her in the face. I crashed into a car that I didn't realize was behind me as a second nigga tossed her in the backseat of the car. Reaching for the door handle, I couldn't get out of my Audi fast enough. The air around me crackled as I jumped out of my vehicle. I took off running as soon as my feet hit the pavement, barely noticing the streets of Milwaukee were beginning to turn a shade of red. Both men hopped in the front seat of their car, busting a U-turn in the middle of the street before speeding off in the opposite direction.

"JORDYNN! WHAT THE FUCK, MAN!"

16

Zane

"You got her?"

"Yeah. She in the back seat, boss man," Boonie replied curtly.

"Bring her out here to the other spot."

"Bet. You got my money?"

"Of course I got yo' money. Have I ever flaked on you before?"

"Just saying, this one a lil' sexier than that last one. You ain't got my money, I ain't dropping her back off. She 'bout to be in Decatur where it's greater," he jeered. "This wifey in the back seat, bruh."

"Just bring her. I got yo' money, my nigga."

"A'ight." Boonie hung up just in time. I'd just walked into the stash house out here in the 'burbs to get Jordynn's ransom money. It was only right that Deo paid for it. Chris too, but the past few months, Deo been the money man, so his contribution was the biggest. Tapping the buttons on the digital safe in the study, I smiled when the green light flashed. Opening the door to all that—air? "The fuck? We got robbed?"

Hitting talk on Chris's number, I practiced that patience thing while waiting the two seconds for him to pick up. "Zane, now isn't the best time to—"

"Oh, you and Deo 'bout to go get our money back? Where y'all at? I'm riding too!"

"Wait, what money? What you talking about, Zane?"

"Ain't we supposed to be meeting up at the stash house today? I'm already out here." I backtracked, forgetting who I was talking to. I didn't make the drops.

"Yeah, but you saying we got robbed? What block?"

"Uhhh—aye, lemme call you back and get the exact details from this lil' nigga." I hung up, hoping he didn't make a few calls to find out what I was talking about. This double life shit was crazy, man.

I unplugged the cameras from this house a while back so Deo and Chris wouldn't see me out here taking money from the stash. I'd ran out of money in my own account from maintaining my current lifestyle after Deo's pops flaked on me that day at the hotel. Pissed off at him and Jordynn, I went and blew 25k in the casino that night and been trying to make my money back ever since. I needed that money, and even with me doing the internet thing myself, I still wasn't making enough to contribute. Steve fucked me up when he took Kim's video off that website. My first check was for 10k. So I'd come out here and get a few thousand out the safe every now and then. Deo wouldn't say nothing about me getting a couple of dollars, but if he found out I'd been grabbing 10k a day for the past month, sometimes 20k a day depending on how my day was going, he might be upset.

On top of that, I was paying Boonie his money out of our stash. I couldn't go pull 50k out of my account because it wasn't there, and the man still had to be compensated for his services. Chris and Deo just needed to understand that our bond as each other's keeper was them maintaining my lifestyle as Zane Stavros until I got back on. I couldn't be out here looking broke. I had a reputation.

The bigger issue was Jordynn. It was gonna take about twenty minutes for Boonie to get to my spot, and I needed to come up with 100k in that time span. "Lemme call Chris back," I mumbled aloud, not knowing what he had going on and not really giving a fuck. "Aye, lil' bro."

"Did you find out who robbed us?"

"Nah, false alarm. Aye, you got any money on you?"

"Not on me, but I can get to some. How much you need?"

"'Bout 100k."

"A hunnit? What you need a hundred thousand dollars for, Zane?"

"Why you questioning me? I can't get 100k off the love?"

"With everything that's happened in the past hour, naw, muthafucka, you can't get shit off the love," Deo's voice growled in my ear. "Where the fuck is my wife, Zane?"

"You married? Aye, congrats, bro. My bad for not getting you and the wife a wedding gift."

Deo chuckled darkly in my ear, and I knew it was about to be a war. "One, two... Deo's coming for you... three, four... gonna kick down your door. Five, six... betta get your shit... seven, eight... be glad you ain't moving weight... nine, ten... never fucking with you again, bitch!" he sang eerily before hanging up in my face.

B: Where you at, my nig?

Me: OMW now

Much money as I already gave him, shit, Boonie should be paying me. I left the house and hopped in the Jag, speeding to the meet-up spot. I wasn't worried about it. What could he do?

"'BOUT TIME YOU GOT HERE, NIGGA!" Me and Boonie shook up in the middle of the street. "I been trying to wake shawty up since we grabbed her, but she must've been tired-tired."

I stepped over to the black Riviera wit' the tinted

windows and peeked in the back seat, taking note of the fresh bruise on her eye. "What's that on her face?"

"Man, yo' brother must be using her as his punching bag or something. I'on know." The nigga with Boonie was quick to speak up first. "You got that bread though?"

"Do I got that bread? Y'all out here beating on my girl, and you asking me 'bout some money?"

"You said snatch her up. That's what we did. Cost extra if you don't want her touched." Boonie stuck a piece of gum in his mouth and looked around absently. "Like my people said, you got that bread?"

"I ain't have a chance to get to the bank—"

"Aye, this nigga ain't got no money. Let's go." Boonie's associate tapped him twice on the arm, and they both walked back to the Riviera. Sliding in the driver's side, I saw the window roll down as he started up the car. "Zane!"

"What—lemme get to the—"

"You can come pick yo' girl up from Decatur, GA when you get me my money. Oh, for every day we have her, it's an extra thou on top of that hunnit." Boonie pulled off without another word, his dual pipes guzzling down the street as the exhaust smoke from his car temporarily clouded my vision.

17

Christophé

"Aye, you think he was following you or some shit?" I questioned my oldest brother. Deo's truck was sitting directly in front of my front steps. He missed the driveway and the garage completely. I thought Jordynn was being extra and not wanting to walk on the concrete, but when he got out the truck, slamming the door so hard it cracked his windshield, I started grabbing the guns.

"It don't e'en matter. All that matters is me blowing this nigga head off, that's it." Deo shoved two pistols on either side of his waist, tucking one in the holster on his ankle before grabbing the keys to his Audi. "Nigga been scheming and stealing this whole time, but I'm the one that's angry when I go choke this nigga out. Yeah, a'ight."

"I'm going too, bro. Zane crossed the line this time. Some shit you just don't do."

We rode out to Zane's townhouse that he didn't know we knew about down in Racine. I had to ride out here with him, because truth be told, we were both ready to kill Zane. Wasn't no talking some sense into him behind this. Jordynn was a sweetheart. She gave me a female's perspective and didn't tell me what I wanted to hear. Jordynn gave it to me blood raw, and I needed that. Once we wrapped up this Zane thing, it was time for me to tell Deo about my son and my baby mama.

"Right here." I pointed at the complex on the right side. "That sign say Lighthouse Point, right?"

"Yeah."

"Yeah, he in the back. Should see that black truck of his or that raggedy ass Jag." Deo looked from left to right as we drove. "There he go."

"You know he parked in front of his house, right?" I checked my pistol to make sure it was still on safety.

"That's ya brother, Mr. "Don't Nobody Know Where I Stay So I'ma Park In Front Of The Spot" face ass." Deo parked four houses down, throwing the car in park. "Let's go see if this nigga want some company."

We crept around the back and hopped the fence. Sliding the metal piece in between the glass doors, we jiggled the lock and heard the click. With the door slightly ajar, we eased the glass aside and crept quietly inside. Even in the upper-class projects, Zane still had Picassos on the wall and cashmere on the floors, which served as a buffer for us to move about the townhouse as we pleased. I found Zane in a bedroom upstairs by himself passed out on the bed naked with a half-empty bag of coke lying next to him. Everything made sense; no wonder he was acting like he'd lost his mind lately.

Texting Deo, I took my pistol off safety in case he decided to wake up and start shooting. "Oh for real? THIS what we doing, Zane!" My oldest brother stepped in the room and looked around with his nose turned up.

"Wha—Deo!" Zane cheered. Jumping to his feet, he stood up and fell flat on his face. "Where Maria at? Somebody need to clean this damn house!" He stumbled to his feet again, gripping the wall for dear life.

"Is that coke on ya nose, bro?" I pointed with my pistol. "Who you copping from?"

"These Kenosha niggas got some great powder, man. We need—" He sniffed and pinched his nose. "We need to link up with them!"

"Zane, I'ma ask you this one time and one time only. You don't answer, and I can't control what happens next..." Deo rested his pistol on our brother's temple and cocked it. "Where Jordynn at, bro?"

"Jordynn?" Zane giggled. "JORDYNN MY NIGGA? You came all the way out here looking for Jordynn?" He roared sardonically. "Yo' bitch—ooops... can't call her that can I? She wifey, right?" He sniffed, pinching his nose and blinking rapidly. His bloodshot red eyes stared at Deo with disgust while he wiped his nose with the back of his hand. "'Wifey'," he whined, "is on her way to Decatur where it's greater." He jabbed a second time.

"Decatur? As in Illinois?"

"As in Georgia, my nigga!" Zane roared. "Them pretty thangs comin' cross tha water... Georgia!" he sang crazily. "Deo, put that gun down fo' you hurt yaself. You ain't gonna do shit! You yo' brother's keeper, right? RIGHT!"

"This nigga high out of his mind." I lowered my piece, seeing the look in my brother's eye. "Didn't you say you can't kill an innocent crackhead?"

"This crackhead ain't innocent." Deo pulled the trigger before I could stop him. Zane's brains splattered like the sun's rays peeking over the horizon on the wall behind him. "Pass me his phone."

I stepped over Zane's body on the floor in a crumpled heap, reaching for his phone on the bed. Deo grabbed it from my hand and unlocked it, scrolling through his text messages before his eyes landed on what he was looking for. "Aye, we gotta pray over this nigga before we go."

"You right." Deo cleared his throat and bowed his head. "Dear Lord, forgive us of our trespasses. Bless us, oh Lord, for we have sinned. And if you see in our hearts that we're out for revenge, please blame it on the son of the morning. Amen."

"Amen. Let's get ghost. It's a long ride down to Decatur."

"Facts." My brother took the silencer off his pistol, reloading while I made sure I had my wallet in case we needed a hotel room. "Think we should call a cleanup crew?"

"Yeah. After all, he is family."

"A'ight." Deo sent a text from Zane's phone to his people, then broke it in half with his bare hands. "Somebody coming to get his ass."

"Let's go."

WATCHING the lights from the city roll by as we drove through Chicago's south side, I figured it was time for me to tell Deo about me and Tandra. Xander was a four-star elite general on the streets, not to mention the only other person Deo trusted outside of us. "Aye."

"Yo."

"Doc let y'all hear the heartbeat?"

"Yeah." He smiled, and I knew that feeling that took over his heart. "That was some crazy shit. I never thought I'd be nobody's father for real, man." Deo cheesed as we passed 95th Street. "Look, Chris, Zane—"

"In all honesty, bro, I understand. Zane tried to make you choose between him and your legacy, and that's some weak shit, for real. Somewhere in his mind, I think he believed that you don't deserve to be happy unless we straight first."

"I think you right, man." Deo merged onto the toll road toward Indiana. "Every time we talked, it was, 'am I my brother's keeper?' Like it was something I wasn't doing, like somewhere I was slacking."

"You know he was saying that shit to me too? I mean, yeah, I fell into the trap for a minute. He got to me. Had me coming at you with that whole 'remember our oath' thing. Aye, bruh, that ain't us. For real, you got your own life to live. It ain't our business what you do with it."

"Jordynn said something like that to her sister before they—" He shook his head before he continued, "Well, you see what happened with them."

"And I see what happened with you and Jordynn. How you stepped up and became your woman's keeper. I'm proud of you, man."

"Thanks, bruh." We rode down the highway both lost in our own thoughts.

"Deo. Bruh, you ain't the only one of us with a baby on the way, man."

"Aw, straight up? Congrats, bro!" He shook my shoulder with one hand. "Who's the lucky chick?"

"Uhmm..."

"Uhmm? I don't know uhmm, bro."

"Tandra."

"Tandra?" Deo pulled to the side of the road and put the car in park. "Tandra who?"

"Man—" I rubbed my hand across my waves before it traveled down my face.

"I'm—Chris, yo' ass too muthafuckin' sneaky for me." He laughed heartily, shaking his head. "Xander know you been rearranging his girl's walls?"

"Shiiit, I don't know how he don't know!" I cackled along with my brother, dapping him up. "You know they fall in love with that Stavros dick. That left hook get 'em every time!"

"BIG facts!" Deo put the car in drive and pulled back on the road. "You telling me I need to kill my top dog? Because if he come for you, I'm coming for him."

"What Zane used to say? 'I got a little brother too'? That's me, bruh. I am Zane's little brother. I ain't worried about X."

"A'ight. Tandra what, five... six months?"

"Yeah."

"Bet. I can't wait, man!" He started beating on the steering wheel again, cackling loudly. "Aye, why we ain't fly out here? This a long ass ride!"

"That adrenaline, man." I shook my head in agreement. "Plus, who gonna pick us up from the airport?"

"Shit, don't you got Waze or some shit on ya phone? Aye, book us on the next flight out of Indy!"

"Man..." I logged onto Delta's website, and it wasn't

nothing leaving until the morning. "By the time that plane land, we'll be there!"

"Yeah, I ain't 'bout to be sleeping in no airport either, so fuck it."

"Aye, wake me up when we get to Kentucky. I'll drive some then."

"A'ight."

18

Jordynn

One minute, I was cussing Deo out, and the next minute, I woke up to the smell of kush and loud music. Two men I never seen before in my life were in the front seat cussing and smoking while the car swerved across...wait, where were we going?

"I GOTTA PEE!" I tried screaming over the loud music, hoping one of them heard me. My face hurt, and I didn't know why.

"What you say, baby? You gotta pee?" the driver questioned, passing the blunt to the passenger before he turned the music down.

"Uhmm... yes. Please."

We came off at the next exit and pulled into a gas station so I could relieve my bladder. I checked the mirror and saw my face was actually swollen. One of these bastards hit me. My stomach started growling when I walked out the bathroom. Deo was supposed to get me something to eat when we left the doctor's office before we got caught up with David.

I grabbed a hot dog off the roller and added some chili and cheese. Since they seemed to think this whole kidnapping thing was cute, one of these men was paying for my food. Deo gave me some money earlier, but that was the least they could do.

"You hungry?" the driver questioned, looking at my hot dog, three bags of chips, two juices, and water.

"Starving. Grab me two Hershey bars with almonds too."

"Eating like you pregnant or something." The driver called himself trying to be funny, pulling out a wad of money. "Gimme this and $25 on pump twelve." He paid for my stuff and got his change before turning back to me. "How you that little eating like that, sexy?"

"'Cause I am pregnant. And even if I wasn't, I got a high metabolism." I took a bite out of my hot dog and walked back to the car.

"You pregnant, lil' mama? For real, for real?"

"Yeah, for real, for real." I opened my own door and was about to climb in the back seat until the driver stopped me.

"Sit up here. I can't have you in the back seat. Aye,

Tariq, apologize to my baby mama for punching her in the face!"

His baby mama? Oh, hell naw— "Uhmm, I need to call my doctor. My stomach been cramping for about an hour." I lied, hoping he'd give me my phone so I could text Deo. I had an app on my phone that I was sure he was tracking by now, but if he wasn't, I needed to let him know to turn the app on.

"You can't take some Tylenol? My first baby mama almost overdosed on some got dammit uhhh... ibuprofen. You can't take that?"

"My pregnancy high risk." I lied again, hoping karma didn't come back to bite me in the ass. "My doctor told me don't take nothing without running it by her first."

"Why you eating all that junk then?" Tariq spat, trying to make me feel guilty for eating chips and candy.

"Look around, Tariq! This ain't Whole Foods! I'm hungry! What am I supposed to eat?" I shot back before biting my chili dog.

"Here." The driver reached in the armrest and passed me my phone. "Make sure you calling the doctor, and don't try no bullshit."

"When it comes to the health of my baby, I ain't got time to be playing these hide-and-seek games with you and nobody else." I opened the messages app on my phone and hit record. "Hey, Dr. Wu. This is Jordynn. I'm calling because I'm having some cramping, and I'm on my way out of town. If you can, call me back with a doctor that

I can go see in—" I pretended like I was hitting the hold button and pressed pause. "Where we at?"

"Right now we in Tennessee, but we on our way to Atlanta." This dummy spoke up first.

"I'm in Tennessee on the interstate, but I'm on my way to Atlanta. Anywhere near I-75 South should be fine. Thanks, Dr. Wu." I hit send and locked my phone before passing it back to him. Hopefully, Deo would make the connection that I was on the highway and turn on that app so he could track exactly where I was.

"So you think your boyfriend Zane gonna get that money up for you?" Tariq questioned from the back seat. "We ain't gonna keep you that long. If he don't call us in three days, you an' that baby gonna be floating in the Chattahoochee."

"What's the Chattahoochee?"

"River. I advise you call your baby daddy," Tariq mocked dryly.

"Zane ain't my man. Who told y'all that?"

"He did." The driver raised his eyebrow, confused. "Wait, do you know who Zane is?"

"Yeah, I know him. He's my brother-in-law."

"Brother-in-law? Deo's *wife*?"

"Oh, so you know my husband?"

"Do I—aye, we ain't going back to Milwaukee, Riq." The driver shook his head as he drove.

"Told you, man! I told you! Ain't shit up there but a bunch of lame niggas and—"

"Uhmm... my husband ain't a lame nigga." I corrected him. "As a matter of fact, Deo Stavros is *far* from lame!"

"You just saying that because you carrying that nigga's seed." The driver waved me off. "All them Stavros niggas ain't worth shit."

We'll see who worth what when my husband show up, stupid muthafucka. "If you say so... I'm sorry, I didn't catch your name."

"Boonie."

"Boonie and Tariq." I pointed at each man to make sure I had their names right for when my husband showed up. They were both idiots. Not only was I sitting in the front seat with the window down letting my hair blow, but Boonie let me use my phone, being all caring and sensitive because I was pregnant. *What if I was lying, dumb ass?* "Why we going to Atlanta?"

"We from Atlanta." Tariq spoke up with his chatty self. "Actually Decatur."

"So y'all kidnap pregnant women all the time down here, huh?"

"For $100k we do."

"Zane didn't give y'all $100k for me?"

"Nah, said he needed more time." Boonie watched the road as he spoke.

"Well, did you call my husband? I know he'll give it to you."

"I'm sure he would—wait, Riq did you call Deo?"

"Nah, we just found out that's her husband. I was trying to get that extra 3k out cha' boy."

"But if that's the case and you thought me and Zane were together, why not just call him to see if he wanted to get his sister-in-law back?"

They looked at each other stupidly. I was over Frick and Frack already. "Uhmm... we got other business with Deo and didn't wanna confuse the two," Tariq stuttered.

"Oh, OK." I turned my gaze back out the window so they didn't see the look on my face. *Oh my God, I wonder if they share a brain too.* "How long before we get there?"

"About four hours." Boonie lit up another blunt and took a long pull.

"Hmph. Never been to Georgia." *I hope I'm there to see what Deo do to y'all dumb niggas when he see my face though.*

"Oh, you gonna like it." Tariq took the blunt from Boonie and started babysitting. "Strip clubs, good food, parties—"

"I don't do none of that, I mostly just hang out with my husband." I huffed, watching the world speed by at 80mph. "Y'all can have all that."

"Aw, we got a real one!" Boonie got hyped, bouncing back and forth in his seat. "Yeah, Ma Dukes gonna love you!"

I wonder if bae gonna kill her too... "Is she cooking?"

"I'll make sure she have you something to eat, pretty face." Boonie touched my cheek, and it took every fiber of my being not to smack his hand off of my face and kick his throat out the side of his neck.

"Thanks, Boonie." I smiled innocently, knowing what they had coming on the horizon. *These duck ass niggas 'bout to get on my nerves.* I rubbed my little heartbeat and... wait... is that a hand? *Oh, baby! Mommy felt that! Deo, my love, where are you?*

19

Kim

I hadn't heard anything from Boonie, Zane, or Deo in the past twenty-four hours, and I was getting desperate. As a matter of fact, nobody seen or heard anything from anybody, which was a surprise. Steven didn't even have any information from me when I went over his house for our weekly date. Yeah, I went over there and told him we couldn't see each other a couple of weeks ago. Rekindling my relationship with Deo was taking longer than I thought, and I was running low on money, so I gave Steve a call.

"Kim, you need to get a job." My mother burst into my room every morning and irritated the shit out of me. "You can't keep laying up round here sleeping all day and out all night."

"I got an interview today." I lied. I wasn't getting no damn job. She talked that same shit every week. I had $3,000 in my purse that I made last night in the club, and the day was still young. Plus, I had VIP at the strip club, which was a guaranteed $5,000. As long as I was living at her spot for the free, I didn't need no job.

"You betta hope they hire you because yo' free ride is slowly coming to the end of the road, hunny!"

"Whatever, Ma. Lemme go get ready for this—Damn, Ma! You just gonna kick me in my fuckin' back?"

"Who you whatevering, lil' bitch!" my mother spat. "Don't start that shit, Kimberly!"

"How I'm supposed to go to the interview with you bruising my damn back!"

"You betta wrap some Saran Wrap around you and go to that damn interview!" she shrieked shrilly. "I mean it, Kimberly!"

"I'm going, damn!" I got up off the steps, snatched my keys off the mantel, and walked out of her house. I was over this free ride already, but when I left her house, I'd be going back to my mansion in Brookfield, thanks to this fake baby.

As soon as I got in the car, I hit talk on Sheena's number. "Whaddup, bitch. Ma Dukes must be pissing you off again, huh?" This hoe knew me too well.

"Girl, I can't wait until I get back home. What you doing?"

"Waiting on these niggas to go home so I can clean this

house. Girl, be glad you stay witcho mama, and she don't let you have company." She low-key called herself coming for me, but I'd still drag her ass all across Milwaukee. "Every night they be over here smoking and shit."

"Hmph, what y'all 'bout to do today?" I started up my car and pulled into traffic.

"Shit. Saw a flyer for this day party yo' boo throwing on IG, so I might go to that."

"My boo? My boo who?"

"Steven." Sheena cackled hoeishly in my ear. "Shit, I'm broke too."

"If that's the case, you should go." I put on my turn signal, then changed my mind. "You can make a lot of money at his parties." I knew what happened at Steven's day parties, hence the reason I stopped going. Plus, we were exclusive... at least we were when I wasn't tied up with David, Ronnie, or Deo. "Aye, what happened with that one thing I asked you to do?"

"Oh, send Deo's wife that sonogram? I did it."

"Bitch, I know you did it," I rubbed the bandage wrapped around my hand. "I'm trying to see if she said something back?"

"Nope."

"Nothing?"

"Nothing."

"Lil' bum bitch. She act like she the only one Deo can get pregnant, like she the only one he fucking—"

"Wait, Deo still —"

"Girl, yeah." I lied. "Regardless of what he do on the street, my baby know where home is."

"Do he?"

"Bitch, whet?"

"I said he shole do! Lemme let you go. I gotta make sure these niggas ain't stealing food out my house. Call me later, boo!" Sheena hurried off the phone.

I needed to get my shit together for real. In order for me to do so, I had to be out of Milwaukee and back in the suburbs where I truly belonged. Instead of my original destination, I hit the expressway and headed toward Brookfield. I didn't care how long it took, I was gonna be there when he got home so we could talk. Maybe he did call me someone else's name the last time we had sex, but today was the day I was telling his "wife" the truth about her husband.

ZANE'S PHONE went to voice mail for the fifth time that day, and I was beginning to get worried. We'd never gone this long without some form of communication, even if it was just a text message. I would've called Christophé, but I wasn't in the mood to be interrogated about how I got his number and why I was calling. I just needed to wait.

My phone vibrated in the cup holder, and I grabbed it before it hit the floor. "Hey, hey, Boonie?"

"Aye, you told this nigga Deo where I live?"

"Did I—no! I don't even know where you live!"

"Where that nigga Zane?" he questioned, sucking his teeth.

"I haven't talked to Zane. Wait, you saying—hello? Boonie?" I checked my phone and saw he hung up.

Me: Where Boonie from?

Stevie: Y U wanna kno?

Me: U not gonna tell me?

Stevie: Georgia.

Georgia? Deo in Georgia?

Stevie: U kno U owe me now.

Me: Wat?

Stevie: Cum to tha house.

I knew I should have waited to text him. Sometimes Steven was so... ugh.

K: OMW.

20

Deo

"Damn, I needed that nap." I yawned, taking a look at my surroundings. The sun was peeking from behind mountains on my right side, and all I saw was trucks flying down the expressway. I wasn't used to this country shit. "Where we at?"

"That sign back there said we about 135 miles from Atlanta." Chris yawned himself. "I'm hungry like a muthafucka. Let's go to Waffle House."

"Boy, what you know about Waffle House?" I tried stretching in the back seat before I gave up. "Pull over, I gotta get out."

"I don't know nothing 'bout Waffle House, but I need some food," Chris replied. "It's a rest stop up here. I'll go there. I ain't trying to get hit by these trucks and be another dead nigga down here on the side of the road."

"Facts." We rode to the rest stop and parked. I hopped out first to stretch my legs. "We gotta get a hotel or something. I smell like yesterday."

"Yeah, and you got ya brother's brains on ya shirt too." He pointed out. "We should've changed clothes. That's why these people looking at us all crazy."

"Fuck these people. They act like they ain't never seen a killer in real life." I pulled my black tee over my head, yanking it off quickly. "My shirt black, so how they know it got blood on it?"

"Blood is thick, and it sticks to cotton, jerk. Should've stopped last night and stretched." Chris chastised me a little as he passed me a clean tee from a brand new pack. "I stopped off at a twenty-four-hour Walmart in Lexington while you was sleep and got us these."

I snatched the shirt from his hand and stretched the neck to give me a little extra room. "Pass me my phone, jerk." Chris tossed my iPhone in the air, and I caught it before it hit the ground. "See if you broke my shit, you'd be paying for it. You are my keeper, right?"

"I ain't Zane. Buy yo' own phone, ol' big-headed ass!"

"Fuck you, jerk," I teased, missing the times when me and both of my brothers talked shit to one another. Unlocking my phone as I walked inside the small building to piss, HER text stood out over all the bullshit, so I hit that one first. Until I saw her face, nothing else mattered to me. "A voice message? Baby..." I stopped in my tracks, putting the phone on speaker as I heard her words flowing from those lips. She was OK for the time being. "On her way to Georgia... cramping? We was just at the... wait, why she keep calling me Dr. Wu? Lemme think... lemme think... doctor... fix? Nah, she know I'ma take care of these niggas. Traveling... damn girl this ain't *Scooby Doo!* Chris!"

"What?"

"Here. Listen to wife message and tell me what she trying to say. I gotta piss." I passed him my phone and headed inside. After answering nature's call, I cupped my hand in front of my face and sniffed my breath. "You need to get to a hotel before you go pick her up, nigga." I spoke to my reflection. "She definitely clowning if she smell that shit!"

I ran my hands under the faucet and wet my face, hoping this water wasn't from the creek or a well behind the rest area. Pushing a kid out of my way, I walked out the bathroom with a little energy, but not much. Yesterday was beginning to catch up with me, but I knew if I went to lay it down, I wouldn't be able to sleep because she wasn't next to me.

"Chris! What she say!"

"You got a tracking app on ya phone?"

"Yeah... shit, you a muthafuckin' genius, Chris!" I snatched my phone from his hand and pulled up the app she made me install. She used to put it on her sister's phone before Journee got hip and started leaving her phone in one place while she was somewhere else. As soon as I opened it, the app showed her exact location. "Daddy gotcha, baby. I'm on my way now, love."

WE GRABBED some clothes from the mall, which I hated shopping at, and checked into the Grand Hyatt. After a shower to wash Zane's blood off of me completely, I took care of my hygiene so I was back feeling like Deo. Soon as Chris finished getting ready, we pulled Jordynn up on the app to see where we were going. "Decatur? Ain't that some shit."

"Well, your brother did say she was in Georgia." Christophé chuckled, patting his pockets for the room key card. "Aye, what you got in the trunk?"

"Come on, Chris, you know me." I scoffed. "These country niggas don't want this smoke."

"Shiiiit, kidnapping sis... yes they do." Me and my brother stepped in the elevator at the same time. Two chicks were in the elevator already molesting my brother with their stares. The situation didn't get any better when I walked in behind him.

"Hello." One of the females spoke up first as the second one raped a lollipop with her mouth. "Where y'all goin'?

"Why? You tryin' to do somethin' wit' them lips? Chris cornered them both as I hit the emergency stop button.

Second chick didn't say a word; she just dropped to her

knees and hooked my brother up. "I'm good." I held my hand up when the first chick headed in my direction. "Wifey would kill me."

"What she don't know won't hurt her though. Anything that happens in this elevator, stays in this elevator," she cooed, rubbing her hand down my chest.

"Bitch, I said no. Go help ya' friend suck my brother up."

I was shocked when she took my advice. I lit up a cigar and watched for a minute before the elevator phone rang. "Yeah?" Chris answered the phone while lil' thotiana gagged on his meat.

"Sir, are you OK? Does anyone need medical assistance?" a voice questioned.

"Mmhmm." He put his hand over the phone's speaker to direct his personal show. "Lick under... right there." Chris moved his hand from the speaker to finish his conversation. "We good."

"Tell 'em you getting ya dick sucked, and they interrupting." I scoffed with my phone on record. He was gonna want to remember this moment.

"Y'all heard my brother. We'll be down there in... shit, girl!" He gripped the wall. I watched as all sorts of shit dribbled from the girl's mouth. "You sure you straight, D? This girl neck game is A1!"

"I'm sure." I hit the button to restart the elevator as the second chick passed her friend a wet wipe from her purse. "Y'all some hoes, ain't y'all?"

"I ain't no hoe." The nasty one started first. "When I see something I like, I go get it."

"Oh, that's what they calling it now, huh?" I sneered before my little brother stepped in.

"Aye, let's hook up later, a'ight? I wanna see you one more time before we go back up top." Chris stroked her face gently.

"OK." She cheesed, exchanging numbers with my little brother just as the elevator stopped.

"Aye, make sure you answer that phone," he called out, balling his lip up and smacking her on all that ass. "Deo, we gotta add a couple more days on the room. You saw shawty an' nem hook me up right there in the spizzot?"

"Christophé, focus. We here for Jordynn, a'ight?"

"I'm coming back out here. Man, I love Atlanta already." He popped the lift gate on the back of my truck, checking under the spare tire for the big-dawg pistols.

We climbed in the truck and hit the streets, pulling up to the address where Jordynn's phone was pinging on the app. I already had the Glock on me. If I needed anything else, Chris had it ready and riding underneath our seats. I parked my truck on the street and walked past the black Riviera that took her away from me almost twenty-four hours ago to the front door and rang the bell. An older lady answered with a polite smile wiping her hands on her apron.

"Hey, can I help you?"

"Yes, I'm looking for my wife, Jordynn?" I questioned,

squinting at the afternoon sun while I rubbed my hand over my waves.

"I don't want no trouble." A frightened looked settled over her face, and I saw her shiver slightly in the doorway.

"Oh, no trouble. Just here for my rib, and I'll be on my way."

"Your rib?"

"Ma'am." I decided to speak to her like I would talk to my grandmother if she was still here. "You ever been married?"

"I have. My husband died three years ago." She looked off in the distance as the memories of her married life no doubt flooded her brain.

"As a married woman, was it the kids, your first house, or that Benz in the driveway that made you love him? Or was it him remembering your favorite soap, you coming home from a long day at work to a home-cooked meal that he made, or getting that 'I love you' text from him when it seemed like everything was going wrong... you know, the small things your husband did for you were what you cherished the most. Am I right?"

"Yup." A small smile tugged at her lips as she heard me out.

"Man... when it comes to my wife, I know that feeling. I miss holding her hand while I'm driving. I miss smelling her hair. I miss putting my hand over her heart while she asleep and realizing that mine beats the same as hers. I been up for the past twenty-four hours because she not next to me. I ain't here to start no trouble, and I appreciate you letting me come to you as a man. Real talk, I just want her back. That's all."

She pulled me in for a tight hug, patting my back while she hummed a melody to herself. "I can't let you go another minute without your rib, son. Jordynn! Your husband is here, hun!"

Heavy footsteps inside the house hit the hardwood floors methodically behind her. A hand appeared and wrapped around her mouth dragging her body backward before the door slammed in my face. *These niggas serious, huh? Good. Me too.*

"Chris!"

"What's good, bruh?"

"Aye, bring me the widow maker."

Chris ducked inside the car and came back with my AR-15 rifle already loaded. "Look, bruh, if they did something to sis, don't forget you got the 4th of July under the third row."

"I gotta see her face. If they tell me she ain't here, then we can make some shit go boom, a'ight?"

"Gotcha, bro."

Dropping the first hollow point in the chamber, I aimed at the front window and started tugging at the trigger. Glass exploded in waves as the window rained tiny slivers throughout the flower bushes in front of the modest house. Pieces of brick ricocheted in clumps on the dirt beneath the bushes, removed in patches from the home's façade.

"AYE, MY MAMA IN HERE!" a voice yelled out from inside.

"Now that I have your attention, I'm gonna say it again. GIVE ME MY MUTHAFUCKIN' WIFE, MY NIGGA!"

"Who the fuck is yo' wife?" a younger feminine voice called out over the tinkering of shards falling from the windowpane.

"JORDYNN! IF YOU IN THERE, LET'S GO!"

"DEO! THEY SAID I CAN'T LEAVE UNTIL YOU GIVE THEM THEY MONEY!" Hearing her scared voice had me on go. I climbed in the window with Chris behind me, both of us with guns in hand.

"JORDYNN!"

Chris's footsteps behind me stopped. I turned to see this nigga Boonie with a gun to my little brother's head. "Deo. You in here shootin' up my mama crib?"

"DEO! THEY GOT A GUN TO MY HEAD, THIS GIRL GONNA KILL ME! BABY PLEASE GIVE THEM WHAT THEY WANT!"

"Look, that's my girl. I know you didn't think I was just gonna let you snatch her up and not come looking for her, did you?"

"Yo' brother said she was his. That's why we got her! She ain't going nowhere until I get my money!"

"How much Zane owe you?"

"A hundred and three thousand dollars, nigga!"

Three? These niggas don't do round numbers? "You gotta let my little brother go. He got the money." Chris and I exchanged glances. He knew what to do.

"Nah, three Stavroses instead of two? Your woman, your baby, *and* your brother? I think the price just went up," the nigga that be with Boonie called out from behind me.

"How much?"

"Three hundred thousand sounds good to me. What about you, Boonie?"

"Three hundred sounds good, but a half a million sounds better." Boonie sucked his teeth, pushing my brother in my direction. "Put the guns down."

We dropped our weapons, and the other dude came and patted us down. "We need our bread, bruh."

"Aye, I got it. I was just about to go meet my folks when I got the call, so y'all can have that." I spoke sincerely. "It's in the truck."

"Go get it. Nah, you know what? We'll all go get it," Boonie insisted, signaling for his boy to follow us out to my truck.

"Chris, gimme the keys. That case still in that one spot?"

"Yeah."

"Bet." The three of us walked to the truck, and they stood next to each other with their guns trained on me as I popped the lift gate and moved the carpet to the side. After shifting the spare tire back and forth a few times to make it seem like I was actually looking for this "case". I grabbed my Ruger and fired two shots in both men before they realized what was going on. Stepping over their dead bodies, I smirked cynically to myself before a second set of gunshots went off inside. "JORDYNN!"

"Deo, take yo' sensitive ass on somewhere. You know I ain't let nobody hurt lil' sis," Chris called out as Jordynn ran from a back room, crashing into my arms.

"I was so scared, Deo! I was so scared!" Her face was wet against my neck. "They were cool until we got here. Then that's when they started acting crazy! That girl pointed a gun at my stomach and said she was gonna..."

"Shhh... it's over, baby. It's over, OK?" I kissed the top of her head.

"Did you get my message?"

"Yeah. Chris had to figure it out. You know I don't be doing all that Inspector Gadget shit."

"Thanks, brother-in-law." She glanced over at Chris with an appreciative smile before turning back to me, running her hand down my cheek. "Baby, you look tired. When is the last time you got some sleep?"

"When I woke up yesterday next to you, pretty girl." I ran my hand through her hair like I always did when I hadn't seen her in a few hours. "We got a room at the Grand Hyatt in Buckhead. Let's go get some sleep."

"Right behind you, love. Chris, you coming?"

"I'll ride back to the spot with y'all, but I'm 'bout to see what my new friend up to." He cheesed slyly. "Call me in the morning."

"Y'all killed that man mama too?"

Jordynn stopped and gave me a deer-in-headlights look. I didn't wanna laugh, but that shit was funny. "Uhmm... Chris?"

"Yes. I put a bullet in mama's head too." He spoke firmly. "That's her kid, therefore a product of her creation. If she wasn't making people with these fucked-up attitudes, she would've been good. You don't bring the game to where yo' mama stay... anything might happen."

21

Christophé

Big bro and lil' sis needed their own space, so I got my own room at the Intercontinental across the street while they slept. I called the chalupa that took care of me earlier, and she came back with the same friend. Oh my God, these ATL thots wasn't no joke! One of 'em even licked my ass. I wasn't expecting that, but I can't say I didn't like it. Now I ain't gay—matter of fact, I'm the furthest thing from it. I didn't ask, and she didn't forewarn me, but that shit felt good.

The sun was way past early morning, looked like it was the middle of the day if I had to guess. Grabbing my phone as soon as my text ringer went off, I pushed thot number one's head off my morning wood and checked my phone. "Aye, move, bitch. I gotta go."

"Hmm... Craig, I thought you said we was going to breakfast at that one place?" thot number two questioned. Breakfast? They didn't even know my real name.

"Y'all need an Uber or something?" I shoved them both off of me, heading to the bathroom with my wallet and my pistol to take care of my hygiene.

"Wait... you not taking us home?"

"No. I didn't pick you up, did I?"

"Aw, *hell* naw!" one of them screamed from inside the room. "Hell naw! Craig, you told us last night that you 'had' us! Now we can't even get a meal?"

"What? You bitches hungry? It ain't eleven o'clock yet, but if you hurry, you can still get a carton of orange juice and a muffin from the continental breakfast in the lobby." I smirked, walking out the bathroom. "Might even be able to still get one of those small boxes of Frosted Flakes. That 'one place' is downstairs."

"You ain't shit, Craig!" Thot number two snatched their clothes from around the room, hopping on one foot as she pulled her leggings back on. "Come on, girl! Let's go!"

"I ain't shit, but both of y'all sucked my dick in the elevator while my brother watched, and you licked my ass. Y'all ain't known me twenty-four hours, but *I'm* the one who ain't shit? Y'all some comedians, for real."

Thot number one turned bright red with embarrassment as thot number two picked up the lamp from the table and tried to throw it at me, dropping it on the floor instead. "We the comedians, but you fucked both of us without a condom. How you know we ain't got herpes?"

"Or maybe we trannies. This is Atlanta," thot number one added, smiling brightly.

"I ain't trying to hear that shit. I know fake titties when I feel them, and if either of you gave me anything, I'll be back. I know where you hoes live."

"How you know—"

I was sick of playing guess who with two bitches whose time with me ran out when the sun came up. These hoes were overstaying their welcome. "How you know I live in Milwaukee? For all you know, that man with me wasn't my brother, and I could live right around the corner! Guess we both gotta find out on our own, huh!"

They rushed out the room together, slamming the door behind them. Going back to my phone, I pulled up Tandra's message and reread it for a second time before I responded.

T: Christophé, I'm so confused. X rubs my belly every morning before he leaves, and every morning, I wish more and more that it's your touch.

Me: I know, T. I miss you and lil' man too. What you wanna do?

T: We can't keep doing this. X deserves to know. He's a good man.

Me: I don't want to put you in a position where you may have to defend yourself, and I'm not there. You carrying my baby.

T: Come over.

Me: Can't. I'm in ATL.

T: ATL? I wanted to go!

Me: LOL, me and Deo came down here on business.

T: When you coming home?

Me: Come out here.

T: Boy, you crazy. X will kill me.

Me: And I'll kill him.

T: Gotta go. Love you.

Me: Love U more.

It was crazy how Tandra and I hooked up at the comedy club. I was there meeting a client with one of the women who worked for me, and she was there with none other than Xander. Deo called him to make a run, so he left Tandra with us. Not too long after, Lynise's date showed up, and she was gone, leaving me and Tandra at the comedy club together. Dave Chappelle showed up that night and shut the whole spot down. Tandra and I kept retelling his jokes to one another long after he left.

Instead of me dropping her back off at home, we rode around for a while talking about life. I didn't open all the way up to her about my past, but there were some things I shared that my brothers didn't even know. In turn, she told me about her life as a porcelain doll for the city's second-in-command. Before X would leave for the day, he'd drop her off promptly at Zane's, then either send a Lyft for her or come pick her up himself. She wasn't allowed to go anywhere without checking in first. He claimed it was because he needed to know she was safe. According to Tandra, he wanted to keep her so safe that she was beginning to question their whole relationship and whether or not she should be in it. I still remember the melancholy expression on her face as she explained what a day in her world was like.

"Do you have someone, Chris?"

"Not really. I can get pussy if I needed it, but for the time being, I'm good."

"Well, hypothetically speaking, if you did have someone, would you make her stay in the house 24/7, only place she allowed to go is to work for your boss's brother?"

"Zane tried —"

"No, Zane treats me like his sister." She interrupted. "What I'm saying is how do you feel about a woman having the freedom to come and go as she pleases?"

"Well, I don't comment on the next man's relationship; that's a female trait. But if the woman was mine, she could do whatever she want. She grown. I know me. She'll be back."

"How you know?" She showed all thirty-two of her teeth in my direction with a curious gleam in her eye.

"That ain't yo' business, but know that I know." I smirked in her direction.

"Christophé, can I be honest with you?"

"Always keep it a buck with me, T. What's on your mind?"

"I used to have the biggest crush on you when I was in high school." She giggled shyly, lowering her head a little.

"Crazy thing is, I had a crush on you too when you was in

high school. I didn't come at you because I heard you was shooting 'em down left and right!" I admitted, snickering more to myself than her.

"Why are you single, Chris? Do you not see yourself with anyone, or is it that you don't want to be with anyone?" she questioned honestly.

"Real talk, I always said if I was gonna do it, I was gonna do it right."

"What's 'it'?"

"Wife, kids, home... all that stuff. I never wanted to be a serial dater or have women running in and out of my life like that. The woman who I ultimately gave my time to would be the woman that I would always give my time to. She deserved that and more from me if I was asking her to give me her love, trust, and soul."

"And have you found her?"

"I thought I did back in the day, but—"

"But what?"

"Then she started kicking it with Xander, and I was back to the drawing board." I divulged after all these years. Tandra blushed before she turned away from my serious glance. She asked, and I spoke my truth.

I was always in love with Tandra. She was voted most athletic, most likely to succeed, and best dressed in high school —all accolades that she'd earned, plus more. I was drawn to her beautiful soul before I was attracted to her beautiful flesh, and by the time I decided to shoot my shot, Xander already swept her off her feet. I was happy for Deo's people, but in my eyes, he had my woman. Even then, I didn't take the Zane route.

"Xander is suffocating me. I don't hate him; I just wanna be happy for a few hours..." She spoke out of nowhere. "Is it wrong for me to get some air for a while?"

"Tandra, I told you before, I'm not the relationship whisperer. What I will say is that you grown. If you not happy, do something about it. Make yourself happy. He'll see it and either get on board or get left. Simple as that."

She gazed sincerely in my direction. Her eyes made me wonder what was going on behind her comforting, brown orbs. "That simple, huh?"

"Yeah—mmm..." Tandra leaned over the arm rest and slipped her tongue in my mouth. Instinctively, I gripped the back of her neck in case she changed her mind. "You sure you wanna do this?" I questioned when we came up for air.

"Just for a little while, OK?"

"Come to my house."

"Does Xander know where you live?"

I didn't care about how Xander felt. If he pulled up to the spot, that's it. She was more of my main focus than anything. "Turn off your phone."

Tandra did as I asked, and I did something that night that I'd never thought to do with anyone... I made love to her. When we got to my house, I carried her upstairs and laid her down on my bed. Her body was nothing short of a work of art spread across my dark-gray comforter. I kissed her everywhere from the top of her head down to her ankles, then back up to French *kiss her irresistibly damp mound. I slipped inside of her gently and asked if she was OK as we shared each other. We were so caught up in the moment that by the time we realized we hadn't used any protection is when I was emptying my seed deep in the cradle of her creation.*

I knew she was pregnant by me because Deo and Xander went down to the DR for a few weeks to iron out a better deal on the dope. Tandra spent those three weeks at my spot, and when Deo called to tell me they were on their way home, I dropped her back off at her place. A few weeks later, she called and told me not only had she missed her period, but the last time she and Xander had been together was a few weeks before her regular cycle last month. Xander thought the baby was his, but after I took her to her first ultrasound, she knew the baby belonged to me.

And now, here we were six months later.

22

Jordynn

Seeing Deo and Chris show up to that house down in Atlanta was nothing short of a gift from God. After they saved me, Chris dropped us off at the hotel and went on about his business while Deo and I got some much-needed rest. I hadn't realized we slept the rest of the day and all of the night away until we woke up with the sun peeking over the horizon.

"Mmm... you OK, love?" he questioned as I stretched myself awake. "How's my baby?"

"We're fine." I smiled at the touch of his hand rotating in circles around my small belly. "How are you?"

"Better now that I got you back." Deo pecked me on the cheek before getting up to go take care of his hygiene. "Did you get your vitamins while we were at CVS?"

"No, I forgot. Can you grab me some for now? I'll get the prescription filled once we get home."

"Don't worry about the prescription. I want you to get them from Dr. Sebi's website. Not trying to expose my baby to all those fillers and chemicals they be putting in these vitamin supplements nowadays."

"Who is Dr. Sebi?"

"Herbalist. Came up with the cure for a lot of these diseases that people out here taking all this medication for, and it's poisoning their bodies yet feeding the disease. Nah, we ain't got time for that because you carrying a king." Deo kissed my belly once he came back in the room.

"Deo, I told you I'm carrying a queen."

"Wanna bet? I got half a million dollars that say I'm right."

"I got half of ten dollars that say you wrong." I returned his cheek peck before going to take care of my own hygiene.

"I want my money in the delivery room, too. Don't be trying to renege!" he called out from the other side of the closed door.

"Boy, you are so crazy! Did you get my phone?"

"Where's your phone?"

I opened the door to the bathroom and stood in the doorway staring at him. "It was in the glove box inside the black Riviera."

"Naw, I didn't know it was in there."

"You think—"

"Hurry up and get dressed, baby." Deo grabbed his phone and dialed a number putting it on speaker. Whoever he was calling didn't pick up, so he called three more times with the same response. "Where's the remote to the TV?"

"Right here." I passed it to him after I pulled my dress over my head. "Deo, what's wrong?"

He ignored me, hitting the power button on the remote and scrolling quickly through the channels. "I just hope these people—"

"We interrupt your regularly scheduled programming to bring you this breaking news from out of Decatur. A local resident discovered an entire family murdered in their home early Sunday morning. Police have no leads and no witnesses, but the local resident who found the bodies had this to say:"

"We's a peaceful people round here, know what I'm talmbout? This a peaceful neighborhood. Ms. Hattie Mae ain't never had nothing but a kind word for everybody that she ever knowed, know what I'm talmbout? E'rybody loved Ms. Hattie Mae. Whoever did this to these nice folk ain't nothin' but the devil, you heard me? I say nothing but the damn devil!"

"Reporting live from Decatur, I'm Jovita Moore with Channel 2 Action News. Back to you in the studio."

"Baby, we gotta go before they find your phone. You damn sure ain't gonna be locked up in no Georgia jail for questioning, and I ain't trying to be in one either."

"Where's Chris?"

"Chris can take care of himself." He shot a quick text

no doubt to his brother before he checked the room one last time for our stuff. "We should have just burned that house down. Shit!" he grumbled more to himself than me.

"I'm ready."

"A'ight, babe. Let's go."

23

Kim

"Breaking news out of Racine County: body parts of what appears to be an unidentified male washed up on the south shore of Lake Michigan today. Sources from the scene tell Fox 6 News that it appears the victim died from a single gunshot wound to the head. Police are asking that anyone with information on this heinous crime contact the Racine Police Department at 262-886-2300. Back to you in the studio."

Steven gave me some money to get my own place once he saw the bruise on my back from my mother's doing. I was seriously thinking about taking his advice. I didn't need to be in the house with her. Even now, with me sitting in the living room watching the news, she was staring at me out the corner of her eyes with her nose turned up.

"Kimberly."

"Yes, Mama?"

"You ain't take out the trash last night." She sucked her teeth, rolling her eyes across the room and back.

"Wasn't no trash in the garbage when I left last night, Mama."

"Well, it is now. How you think it got there?"

I took a deep breath in and blew it out slowly counting to ten. "Mama, I don't know."

Before I knew it, she jumped up and grabbed me by my ear, pulling me off the couch toward the kitchen. "You disrespectful as shit, Kimberly! Look in this can! Look at it! See all that trash, Kimberly! See that shit! That's what you left in this kitchen to funk my house up! I came down here this morning, and the whole kitchen smelled like trash!"

"Mama, it ain't nothing but two candy wrappers in here!" I yelled out, teetering over the small can. She had a firm grip on my ear, twisting it back and forth. "Let me go, dammit!" I tried to pry her hands off of me.

I was caught completely off guard when her hand came up from nowhere and whacked me in the face. "Bitch, you think you grown, huh! Yo' lazy ass gotta go! You ain't 'bout to be in my house sleeping all day and partying all night while I'm breaking my back to work and keep this house clean behind you! I don't care about you not having nowhere to go! Get the fuck out, Kimberly!" My own mother pushed me to the floor as if I was some random in the street and she didn't birth me.

I hopped back up and got in her face. I was sick of her

accusations about what I wasn't doing, knowing I was breaking my back to do everything she wanted before she asked so I didn't have to hear her mouth. "What have I ever done to you?" I demanded to know. My mother had her days, but it seemed like the older I got, the more vindictive she became. "You gave birth to me, so I don't understand why you hate me so much!"

"I never wanted you, Kimberly! I only had you because your father was married, and his wife told him she wasn't having no more kids after she gave him a son. He stopped giving me money for you when you were a baby because his wife found out about us and threatened to leave. All that shit he talked about how much he loved me... hmph! Love didn't make him stay either! I tried giving you to the state, but they said they would put me in jail for neglect, so I kept you! I begged your father to take you at least for a couple of months, but he said no! I hate Steven for what he did to me!" she spat through gritted teeth.

I couldn't have possibly heard her correctly. "Steven? Mama, I thought you said my father's name was James?" A loud thumping noise began to beat inside my head as the rest of my body froze.

"Girl, James was the man I been fucking since you was a toddler. He was taking care of us. Why wouldn't you call him daddy? Bitch, have you looked at your birth certificate?" Per usual, she felt the need to insult me when all I asked was a simple question.

"Mama, ain't nobody listed on my birth certificate as my father! Who is Steven?"

"Hmph! Just because we wasn't married don't make him no less yo' real daddy." She sucked her teeth and turned her nose up again. "Your real father is Steven Pembrooke, owner of the—"

"STEVEN PEMBROOKE! Mama, I—oh my God. OH MY GOD!"

"Oh your God what, Kim? Don't be trying to go up to his job and ask for no money! He gonna tell you no! I already tried it, for your information!"

"Did—Mama, how do you know Steven Pembrooke is my father? Did—did you do a DNA? Mama, how do you know!"

"I know because I know where my pussy been!" she screamed in my face as we stood nose to nose. "Plus, the asshole had me do a DNA, so that's how I know!"

"I gotta—I gotta get out of this house..." I grabbed the counter for support. My legs felt wobbly as my brain processed what I'd just been told. "I-I can't..."

"That's what I been telling you this whole time! Get out my house!" she yelled from behind me as I grabbed my keys and ran out her house.

This whole time... all the things we've done... this whole time... I started out having sex with my brother, then graduated to my own father? My stomach rumbled for a second before everything I'd ate in the past twenty four hours moved quickly up my throat and spewed from my lips.

"Don't leave that in front of my house, girl! Getcho ass back here!" her voice hollered from the porch as I started up my car and sped off down the street.

DRIVING 90 mph to get to Steven's condo, my mother's words played in a fractured loop over and over in my head. *Your real father is Steven Pembrooke... Your real father is Steven Pembrooke... Your real father is Steven Pembrooke...* My real father had been...oh my God. The thought alone had me dry heaving on the side of the road. I couldn't believe I never noticed the resemblance between me and him. Why do people keep secrets like this from their families? Why didn't I know about this before now? Why am I throwing up all over... oh my God... *We never... what if... what if I am... He never wore a fucking condom... Steven said he had a vasectomy... oh my God...*

"Steven!" I hopped out of my car with the ignition still on and ran to his townhouse. "Open this door, dammit! Steven!"

"Shhh... Kim, what is wrong with you?" He nudged me away from the door, shushing me in the process. "My wife is here, and she's sleeping. What's so important that you had to come over here now?"

"Your wife is here? Oh, lemme come in so we can have

this conversation as a family then!" I moved him out of the way, barging inside.

"Kim, what are you—oh yeah." He stopped and covered his mouth as we both heard rustling from upstairs. "You're... damn, what was her name?"

"Kyana." I was stunned at the fact that he didn't even remember my mother's name, considering they had a child together.

"Kyana's daughter. Yeah. I took that pussy when she was young, did she tell you I was her first?" He snickered contemptuously. Now it made sense why my mother was so upset that he didn't want her. But she had me the day after her sixteenth birthday...

"Steven, I miss you," a woman's voice sang from the steps. "Who was at the—Kim?"

"Sheena? Really?"

"Go back upstairs while I take care of this situation, OK?" He soothed her, kissing her cheek while patting her ass. Sheena and I exchanged glares before she walked slowly back up the steps with a small smile on her face. *This jealous bitch can't keep her legs closed for shit.* "Now, Kim, how was I supposed to know—"

"Maybe if you'd been in my life, you'd know who I was!" I shot back, feelings of shame and embarrassment flooded my soul. "Do you know what we've done, Steven? What I've done with my own brother!"

"You got some good pussy too, just like your mother

did." He moved closer to me and caressed my face with the back of his hand.

"STEVEN!"

"Look, ain't nothing we can do about it now. The damage has been done, right?" He moved closer still, his lips hovering just outside of mine. "Why you making such a big deal about it?"

"Why am I making such—are you serious!"

"All it means is that every time you called me daddy, you weren't just playing a role. Now I know for sure you care about me."

I backed away from him. The room started spinning slowly at first, then twirled faster and faster as he stood in my face smiling crazily. "Oh my God... Steven, I can't believe..."

"You can't say I ain't never took care of you. I been giving you money for the last five years." His face contorted into a blur. I saw his teeth grinning at me like a Cheshire cat with his voice echoing in my ears. "Nobody has to know but me and you. We don't have to talk about this ever again, sweetie. Let's put this small faux pas behind us."

"Faux pas? Is that what I am to you? A faux pas?" I could barely get a whisper out with the pounding headache from earlier creeping back up my neck.

"Kimberly—" The last thing I saw before I fainted was his hands reaching out to grab me so I didn't hit the floor.

24

Deo

I'd been lying low since we had to get the fuck out of Atlanta a month ago. Jordynn was getting bigger by the day, and I loved every minute of it. We went to the ultrasound, and for an hour this baby showed us everything but whether he was a boy or girl. I knew then it was a boy; only a Stavros man was that damn stubborn. Every day, wife was texting me with something else crazy she had a craving for. It had gotten to the point that I dropped her off at Christophé's and gave him money to cook whatever she wanted. Her lil' fat butt was happy then.

Journee's funeral was small; only me, the wife, and Chris were there for the service. Even still, I had her transported from the funeral home to her gravesite in a glass carriage pulled by two white Clydesdale horses with a black coachman dressed in all white. Never in the city's history did a crackhead have a bigger funeral procession than Journee Young. People came out of their homes just to watch her casket move down the street. The whole hood came out and paid their final respects to my sister-in-law, as they should have.

Chris and Tandra were still sneaking around the city whenever they could. That night he told me about him getting her pregnant had me stuck because Xander treated that girl like she was Snow White, and he was the only dwarf. She got a little freedom when she worked for Zane, but when that doctor said bed rest for a few weeks, he took that shit way too far. I think what they meant was that she couldn't be outside in all that weather, but X said she was staying in the house until her due date. Surprisingly, my brother allowed it. He didn't want her overly excited while she was pregnant. If I knew Chris, wasn't nobody or nothing stopping him from being in that delivery room when the time came. I was already looking through the team to see who could step into X's place once I dropped him in a patch of concrete in a few months. I had some time.

Zane's body parts had been washing up on the lake for the past few weeks. They found his torso the other day. My people said they were still missing one of his legs, three of his fingers, and a hand. Chris filed a missing person's report the day he got back from Atlanta so we weren't implicated in his death. The property management company contacted us to give their condolences and let us know his apartment was a crime scene, as if we didn't already know that. Once the police gave them the all clear, they'd call us back to clean his stuff out the spot.

Kim called me earlier today saying we needed to talk, and I was ready to hear her out. I still hadn't found out who sent wife that message, but at this point, it didn't matter. Me and Jordynn were in a good place in our relationship where she trusted me, and vice versa. I told her to come by the house by two o'clock. That way, I had time to run over to Chris's spot and pick the wife up. I didn't need no crossed lines, no insinuations, no messages, nothing. Jordynn was petty as hell. I was still finding those screenshots in my closet a month later.

Jogging up the steps in front of Chris's house, I was just about to tap in the code when the door swung open. Jordynn stood in the doorway with a sandwich in one hand and her purse in the other. "Hey, baby daddy. You ready?"

"Baby daddy, huh?" I leaned in and kissed her neck, checking out the outfit she had on. Baby looked sexy as hell as always, dressed in an all-white, form-fitting dress that hugged her like a glove, showing off our baby bump. I'd just bought the gray Dolce and Gabbana leather biker jacket hanging around her shoulders while we were on our way back from Atlanta, only because she convinced me it matched her gray stilettos perfectly. Jordynn knew I loved her hair straight down her back, and I promptly ran my fingers through her strands.

"I don't recall saying 'I do', so that makes you my baby daddy." She kissed me on the lips, heading for my truck. I ran ahead of her and grabbed her door, making sure she was comfortable before I closed it.

"So I get yo' lil' dusty ass seven carats, and that don't mean shit, huh?" I hit the push button start and pulled out the driveway.

"Seven carats? This a cubic zirconia, boy whatchu talking about?" She raised her hand and wiggled her fingers in my direction.

"This ain't." I reached in my pocket and passed her a ring box. Pulling over on the side of the road, I leaned over and wiped the tears streaming down her face. "Oh, now we quiet, huh?" I grinned, watching as her hand shook slightly.

"Deo... you make me so sick." She opened the box slowly and wept harder. "This is so beautiful, baby."

"Am I baby daddy, or am I baby? I'm confused, big mama." I took the box from her and took the ring out, sliding it on top of the two carats I originally gave her when we got back from Atlanta. My jeweler was out of town, and that was all I had access to at the moment.

"You baby. You my baby, Deo." She showered my face with kisses before she tried to climb over the armrest, but Junior stopped all that. "I'll thank you when we get to the house," she purred, rubbing my mans through my jogging pants.

"Uhhh... about that. Jordynn, I got something to tell you."

"Deo, don't make me slap you. Can this wait? Lemme enjoy my new ring, damn!"

"I came to pick you up because I don't want Kim coming at you or sending nobody to come for you." I pulled back onto the street and headed for our home.

"Why would she do that?"

I took a deep breath in and blew it out slowly focusing on the road. "Jordynn, you know I love you, right?"

"Why would Kim come for me, Deo Stavros?"

"You uhmm...you remember back when we uhhh... when you was at Potawatomie?"

"Go on."

"Kim, uhhh... baby, one day we gonna look back at this whole thing and laugh about it..."

"We ain't laughing about it today though. What did you do, Deo?"

"I love you, Jordynn. That ring alone should tell you how much I love you... We got a whole baby..."

"DEO, WHAT THE FUCK DID YOU DO!"

"I swear I didn't do nothing, love. She, uhhh... she..."

I pulled up to the house not expecting to see her car parked in front of the gate. This bitch was fifteen minutes early. *Damn*, I whispered under my breath.

"Tuh! Too late. Yeen gotta tell me nothing. I'll ask this hoe myself." Before I could stop her, Jordynn was out the truck, charging toward Kim's car. "Open this muthafuckin' door, bitch! What I tell you last time you came to my house! Come take this ass whipping like a muthafuckin' woman!"

I wrapped my arms around her waist and picked her off her feet, carrying her back to the truck. "What the fuck is wrong with you, girl! You pregnant! You ain't supposed to be out here fighting and shit! What if something happen to my baby!"

"*Your* baby?" Kim wobbled out of the driver's side of her car. "What about *our* baby?" she proclaimed proudly, rubbing her small baby bump.

"Oh, so *you* the one that sent me that 'Congrats, step mama' bullshit! Betta go get you some welfare to help you take care of that baby cause he'll never see it!"

"Kim, listen—" I put my arms out to hold both women at bay. This wasn't gonna go well.

"No, Deo, *you* listen!" she screamed. "You promised me that last night we made love that you'd be there for me and our child! Now you got this bitch—"

"'Made love'? We wasn't making love when you lived here, much less when you didn't! Aye, what the fuck you on, man?"

"Oh, now you don't remember?" She smiled slyly. "That day a few months ago when I came over to get my stuff? You told me you loved me! You promised you'd—"

"I told you—"

"Deo Constantine Stavros, what the fuck is she talking about?" I ducked because I knew she was swinging on me behind my back.

"Constantine? Your middle name is Constantine?" Kim pointed and laughed at me. "I know you half Greek, but damn! Your mama should've fucked a black man because Constantine is NOT sexy!"

Before I could stop myself, I caught her around the neck and choked her out on the hood of her car. "What did I tell you that day in the basement, Kim? Huh? What the fuck did I tell you, Kim!"

"Bitches... bitches bleed... Deo, please..." She clawed desperately at her neck.

"Bitches bleed... finish it. Finish it, dammit!"

"Bitches bleed just like us..." She wheezed.

"I'll murder a pregnant hoe too. Don't forget that." I leaned down and whispered in her ear, finally releasing her from my grip. "Get the fuck outta here, Kim."

"Yeah, beat it Kim!" Jordynn picked up a brick from near the front gate and threw it at Kim's head, connecting perfectly with the back of her skull. "Deo, let's go!"

I made sure Kim made it back to her car. I might not have a relationship with her, but if she died, that was another problem on my hands. Jordynn already killed one person with that right-handed swing of hers. She didn't need to be catching two bodies. "Go straight to the hospital. Call me and let me know what's going on with you," I whispered quickly, kicking her car door.

"Fuck y'all whispering about, Deo! I got another brick in front of my house! Play with me! PLAY WITH ME, DEO!"

"Jordynn calm down—"

"You fucked her, Deo? While I was in the hotel, Deo, you fucked this bitch? You fucked this bitch while I was at the hotel, Deo?"

Jordynn had the lingo to ask me the same question five different ways, and from the look in her eye, I knew if I didn't answer her and it had to be a sixth, she was gonna swing on me again. "Baby, I swear this wasn't supposed to happen. She sucked my—"

"Oooohhh, she sucked your lil' ding-a-ling, huh! Just like I said! Let me the fuck out this truck!"

"Wait, Jordynn!"

"Let me go!" She wiggled out of my grip and took off running. I took my time getting out the truck because no matter how mad she was at me, Junior was gonna stop her from getting too far. "Deo, come get me off these damn steps!"

"Oooohhh, fat mama can't run, can she?" I couldn't help but tease her sitting on the steps mad and wheezing, trying to catch her breath. "Come on, baby."

"I'm still mad at you." She punched me in my kneecap before accepting my outstretched hand. I picked her up and cradled her in my arms, carrying her to the front door. Tapping in the code for the house on the keypad, the door swung open, and I took her inside, placing her down gently on the couch.

"Listen to me. Yes... I'm not gonna lie to you, yes. Kim and I fucked while you were at the hotel. This ain't no excuse for why, but I had been drinking, and she claimed she wanted to talk. But if she told the truth, you'd know she asked me to tell her I loved her, and I told her I love you. Come on, Jordynn. She had to suck my dick to get me hard. Do that sound like I'm in love with Kim?"

"You could be..." She dropped her head and looked away.

"But I'm not. You ain't never sucked my shit, and you pregnant. What that tell you?"

"Is that what you want?" she questioned lowly.

"I don't want anything you don't want to give me. You ain't gotta prove nothing to me. You already wearing my ring and full of my baby. I'm good."

"Promise?" She scooted closer to me and rested her head on my shoulder.

"I promise. I'll kill a muthafucka over you. You my heart."

"I know. They still ain't found who killed Miss Hattie Mae an' nem down in Decatur." Jordynn burst into a fit of laughter, playing with my earlobe.

"Yeah, they ain't even looking either. Ya man know people that know people." I kissed the top of her head. "Aye, that was your brother-in-law that murked Ms. Hattie Mae and that girl, not me."

"Oh, you didn't leave Boonie and Tariq in the driveway, huh?" She looked up at me with those slightly slanted eyes.

"Boonie and Tariq left themselves in that driveway. I don't know nothing about all that. I was at the hotel in Buckhead with my lady." I met her lips halfway, brushing a soft kiss across her thickness.

"Deo, I love you."

"I love you too, big mama." I touched my forehead to hers, lost in her brown orbs. "I seem to remember somebody saying they was gonna thank me when we got home."

"Come upstairs in five minutes." She smiled deviously, climbing the stairs one by one. "Bring me a bottle of water too. I can't be flipping off the chandelier and twerking on the four-poster bed for you no more."

"Tie me up, and ride it then, like you did that one night!" I called out once she made it to the top, hurrying inside our bedroom.

I reached for my phone to put it on do not disturb when I saw a text from Kim. Glancing upstairs to make sure Jordynn wasn't watching me with a glass vase in her hand, I opened it up to read:

2627963798: CAT scan didn't show any damage. Doc said I had a bruise, but it wasn't too bad. They stitched my head and gave me some ibuprofen for pain because of the baby.

Me: Thought U wasn't pregnant.

2627963798: I am. X sent U the test.

Me: He said Boonie sent that from his phone.

2627963798: U saw me

Me: I'll pay this bill, but I ain't paying for no kid until I get a DNA. Hit the jack when U ready.

2627963798: I really need to talk to U, Deo. It's important.

Me: About?

2627963798: Can I C U without your "wife"?

Me: I'll let U kno.

"Deo, it's been seven minutes! I'm 'bout to go to bed!" Jordynn called down the steps.

Switching my phone to do not disturb, I shoved it behind a couch pillow and went upstairs to get thanked, hopefully the rest of the night, if Junior wasn't being a hater.

25

Christophé

I left Jordynn at the house. Tandra called and said she was having some cramping, so we had to go get that checked out ASAP. My baby boy had eight more weeks before he was due to make his entry in the world, and he needed to cook as long as possible. Tandra seemed a little depressed lately. If she wasn't going to her appointments, X didn't want her going nowhere. She had to open the window to get some air, let him tell it. Doc was concerned because she wasn't getting enough exercise, but you think that nigga cared? Hell naw. So when big bro texted me letting me know he was on the block, I went over his house and picked her up so she could do what she needed to do.

"Since you're around thirty-two weeks now, I believe the cramping you're experiencing is the normal stretching of your ligaments that women experience during their first pregnancy. You don't appear to be in active labor, just monitor your pain and come back if it worsens or you feel a sudden gush of liquid or see bleeding. However, Tandra, I'm looking over your blood work, and I gotta admit I'm worried about your eating habits. Are you getting enough iron in your meals?" Dr. Webster questioned, reviewing her chart.

"I eat, but I haven't been taking my prenatal vitamins as much as I should," she admitted sadly.

"Why not, dear?"

"My, uhmm... my boyfriend hasn't been able to get to CVS to pick them up for me."

"Mr. Stavros—"

"Nah, Doc. She ain't talking about me." I nipped that in the bud quick. I ain't no deadbeat. "Now that I know she out, I'll take care of that pronto. She need to be making sure my baby got what he needs to grow."

"I didn't think you were aware." Doctor Webster nodded, reviewing her chart astutely. "But I also know Ms. Grant is in a situation, so I won't pry."

"Thank you." Tandra laid back on the exam table and lifted her shirt. Doctor Webster grabbed the Doppler ultrasound device and poured the gel on my baby mama's stomach. "Let's just make sure baby's heartbeat is strong, and then we can let you go home."

I loved hearing my baby's heartbeat. I would hear his little heart tones in my sleep for days afterward. As soon as she pressed the fetal stethoscope to her baby bump, and the familiar beat came through the small speaker, I knew something was wrong. "Doc, you hear that?"

"Yes, Mr. Stavros, I do. Tandra, we're going to go ahead and admit you as a precautionary measure." Doctor Webster ducked out the room for a second, then returned with a nurse.

"Why? What's wrong—Chris?"

"I ain't no doctor, but his heartbeat sounds irregular to me." I sat her up to fluff her pillow before I helped her lie back down. "How are things at home? X fucking with you still?"

She turned away, staring out the window with her lips pursed together. "Christophé—"

The nurse hooked her up to the baby EKG and another machine that monitored her heart rate. I watched as Tandra's face frowned slightly when she quickly wrapped the Velcro and elastic belt around her to hold the baby Doppler still so it didn't slide off her round belly. Giving us both a tight smile, she nodded before she ducked out the room as quietly as she came in.

"I don't wanna hear that shit about how good of a man Xander is. I wanna know is he fucking with you?"

"Chris, I can't leave him—"

"You can't leave him? So you OK with him putting my baby at risk?" I tried hard not to raise my voice, but she wasn't making no sense. Fuck him! When it came to

Christophé Achilles Stavros III, I'd body his ass today if something happened to my son.

"You wouldn't understand, Chris." She dropped her head and wept. "We lost a baby before, and now I'm pregnant. He's looking out for my best interests by making sure I'm not in a position to lose this one."

"So that's why he locks you up in the house by yourself and tells you that you can't leave? You can't go outside and get some air, and you can't go to the corner and back? You can't even get the fucking mail?"

"I-I think he knows about us." She revealed.

"Why you say that?"

"I woke up one night to go to the bathroom, and he was staring me in the face with tears in his eyes. I asked him what was wrong, and he said... nothing."

"So?"

"Chris... Xander and I have been together since high school. I know this hurts him as much—"

"You know what? I ain't gonna make you choose between me and your high-school sweetheart. I will say this though: you and him ain't gonna be raising my son like he the one that's supposed to save y'all relationship. I'll be damned if I'm gonna stand by like some duck ass nigga and just say, 'OK, baby. You and your man can raise my son.' You got me fucked all the way up if you think that's gonna happen. I'll walk in your house and take him if I have to!"

"Chris, I'm not saying that! I just need time—"

"How much more time you need, Tandra? You had thirty-two weeks to tell him what it is!"

"Chris, he would've made me leave—"

"So? You act like I ain't got a six-bedroom, four-bath house that I live in by myself! Man, save all them excuses and shit. This would've gone a lot different if you would've just got an abortion! I would've paid for that!"

"Chris, are you saying you don't want our baby?" Tandra all of a sudden cared about my seed, like she wasn't just pleading with me to understand how her man felt about me knocking her up.

"Tandra, I *never* said I didn't want our baby. I love my son, and I damn sure want him. I want his mama too. I want you to have the rest of my babies. I ain't trying to have all these different women out here with my kids! What I'm saying is that you want me to sympathize with the nigga that's stressing you out and gave my baby a fucking arrythmia in utero! If he don't make it, I ain't responsible for whatever actions I might take against ya man! Trust and believe that!"

"An arrythmia? In utero? Chris, you been watching *Grey's Anatomy* without me?" She snickered.

"Man, what I'm supposed to do at night? You got me hooked on that shit. Y'all know I don't be in the streets." I cackled with her. She caught me. "Tandra, all I'm saying is that you don't have to go through none of this. I wanna be the one waking up next to you and rubbing your belly. I wanna be the one you cuss out because you want something to eat every twenty minutes. I wanna know all ya crazy cravings. Deo drop Jordynn off at my house for days so I can cook for her. I wanna cook for you too... that way, I know both of my babies eating." I rubbed her ponytail down her back.

"I just feel like there's a sense of loyalty there between me and Xander that I don't want to break. He's been there for me for so many moments in my life that I feel like I owe him. Chris, we were wrong for doing what we did—"

"And still do. You left your panties at my house the other day."

"Oh, that was on purpose. I don't want no bitch laid up in my baby daddy bed." She tucked into her pillow comfortably.

"Bitches ain't allowed at my crib, so you straight." I leaned in and kissed her on her pink lips. "I get that you and him have a past, and that's cool. But you ain't gonna never be happy if you base the future of your relationship on your past. What happened to that cool lil' chick who sat across from me that night and asked if it was OK for her to breathe? Is she still holding her breath?"

"She's breathing now, thanks to you." She smiled with her head bowed.

"That's all I'm saying. You want me to go talk to X? Tell him he ain't gonna be in the delivery room with my baby? Neither of y'all?""

"No, I'll tell him." She spoke with renewed strength to her voice. "I hate to say it, but our relationship has run its course, and we're both holding on to something that really isn't there anymore."

"Do I need to be there?" I didn't know if X ever put hands on Tandra, but I knew he was one of them niggas that couldn't keep their hands to themselves. He'd put paws on a few of my girls before that I had to get in his shit over.

"I'll be fine, Chris. I'll just let him know, and we'll move forward from there."

"Yeah, I need to know when this conversation is happening. Now before you say you got it, I'm telling you again: that nigga can't tell me nothing when it comes to you because you carrying my son. Matter of fact, I'ma call him up here right now." I texted X and told him to come to the hospital because I had something to tell him.

"Chris—no! Why would you do that?" Tandra sat up suddenly, anxiously wringing her hands. She seemed genuinely scared of what X was going to do if he found out.

"I know this nigga ain't hitting you, but what is he doing to you? Tell me, Tandra."

"Chris, he—"

"Aye, I was already in the area when I got ya message, chief." X walked calmly inside the room, looking back and forth between me and Tandra before resting his gaze on her. That was too quick... Was he standing outside the door the whole time? "What's going on?"

"Xander, I—" She trembled with her mouth stuck open as I texted Deo.

"What have you done, Tandra? Hmm? Been hoeing around with these Stavros niggas?" He focused his stare on her neck.

"Look, X—" I began before he put his hand up to shush me. "Nigga, I ain't none of these hoes out here! You ain't 'bout to be hushing me! Now, ya girl got something to tell you!" I looked at her lying on the bed as white as the sheets she was lying underneath when the nurse burst in the room.

"Everyone out now! Her heart rate is off the charts! We *have* to get this baby stable!"

"That's my baby mama! I ain't—" I yelled out as the nurse pushed *both* of us out of Tandra's room.

"Unless you're God, you, him, and nobody else is allowed in that room until that baby's heart rate returns to normal! Now, I don't know what the deal is between you two, nor do I care. But if your presence affects her mental state, it affects baby. If you haven't got the message, that means get the fuck out of this hospital until she calls you and tells you to come back, or I will have you both arrested for child endangerment. Are we clear?"

I looked Xander up and down, sucking my teeth before nodding my head. "Yeah, we clear. Ain't we, X?"

"Mmhmm." He sized me up for a few seconds before sucking his teeth at me. "We good."

"Now, Mr. Stavros, you can take the first elevator, and Mr.... I'm sorry, who are you?"

"Laws. Xander Laws. That's my fiancée you got in that room, so you betta take care of her." He threatened the same nurse who just threatened us. The same nurse who put us out for stressing out my son.

"Mr. Laws, you can take the second elevator."

"I ain't going no muthafuckin' where until I find out why I was called up here in the first place!" Xander roared.

"Nigga, you was already here! What you mean?" I walked up on him before the nurse put her arm out to stop us. "You know why you here!"

"Yolanda, call security. I'm not gonna play referee with these two when there's a baby whose life hangs in the balance!" she yelled out.

"His life?" I stopped, reality punching me in the gut as Xander swung on me...

26

Jordynn

Deo was laid up in our bed curled up in a ball like a newborn baby once I was done thanking him for my ring. That whole Kim thing was inevitable. Deep down, I knew she was gonna come at me talking 'bout "I'm pregnant". Now I know who sent that wack ass sonogram. Based on everything Christophé told me, I didn't know what made her think she was pregnant by Deo.

"Mr. Stavros," I whispered in his ear, giggling when he took me in his arms and pulled me closer to him. "I was gonna cook you something to eat. What are you in the mood for, love?"

"You already know what I want to eat." He nibbled at my earlobe while his hands roamed indolently over my

FatimaMunroe

curves, finally resting on our baby bump. "But what you cooking though?"

"Nothing big, I was gonna fry some chicken and probably some spaghetti, corn on the cob, some rolls..."

"You trying to make me gain this pregnancy weight with you, and I can't." He placed soft kisses on my neck and chest. "I got a reputation on these streets."

"A reputation? As what? My baby daddy?"

"Keep playing with me, Jordynn." Deo bit my nipple, mashing his thick manhood against my middle. "I'ma give yo' ass twins tonight."

"That's not how that works, Deo. That's not how any of that works." I mushed his head before I stood up and headed for the door.

"Well, it should, dammit. That's OK. Next time I'ma get yo' muthafuckin' ass." He threw a pillow at me, and it missed.

I stuck my tongue out at him before I ducked out of our bedroom. Flopping down the circular staircase, I slid across the foyer in my fuzzy socks on my way to the kitchen when I heard something in the living room vibrating. "What is that noise?"

Walking in the living room, I stood in between the ottoman and Deo's favorite chair to listen if I heard the vibrating noise again.

Bzzzzt... Bzzzzt... Bzzzzt...

Moving the couch pillows, I found his phone tucked between the cushions. *What is this man hiding?*

Deo turned the passcode off on his phone a few months ago, so I slid my finger across the home screen, and his notifications popped right up. I ignored everything from the streets, instead tuning in on the messages that kept coming in every few seconds from an unsaved number in his phone:

2627963798: Deo, I know you said you'll let me know, but I just feel like we've been through too much to end like this.

2627963798: Yes, I might've jumped the gun on that whole proposal thing, but can you blame me? Deo, you have been the key to my heart for the past five years now, and nothing? You put me out your house like I'm trash.

2627963798: That whole thing with Zane, I was drunk. He told me to come over, and we started drinking. One thing led to another, and that video happened. Your brother took advantage of me. Did he apologize to you for what he did? I bet he didn't.

2627963798: What can I do that will change your mind? I'll do anything.

2627963798: Nobody loves me, Deo. Nobody. My mother told me she hates me, and I found out Steven is my biological father.

2627963798: Deo, please, call me back. I love you. I love our baby. You don't want Jordynn. You want me. I forgive you. Please, Deo.

2627963798: I'm in that dark place, Deo. You remember, like I was before. It's cold, Deo. I'm freezing.

2627963798: I'm sorry for everything. I never meant to hurt you, Deo.

2627963798: Why are you treating me like this? Does our baby really not mean anything to you?

2627963798: Deo.

2627963798: Deo, please?

2627963798: I'm gonna keep texting until you answer me.

2627963798: DEO!

Ain't nothing worse than a begging ass woman when the man don't want her. I was about to put his phone back when Chris's text came through, saying Tandra was at the hospital, and X just walked in.

"Deo! Wake up! We gotta go!"

"What's wrong, Jordynn?" he called out over the balcony.

"Christophé Achilles Stavros II and III are both at—"

"Tell me in the car." He came running down the steps, pulling a shirt over his head with one hand while tucking a pistol in his waist with the other. "Come on!"

Deo grabbed my wrist and pulled me out the house so fast I didn't have a chance to set the alarm. "Somebody gonna come steal our stuff, babe."

"Pull up the Brinks app and hit lock. We'll be a'ight." He sped off down our half-mile driveway to get to the street. "Where's my brother and nephew?"

"ProHealth in Waukesha." I spoke quietly.

"ProHealth in Waukesha? Why they at ProHealth in Waukesha? Nephew only seven months in."

"I don't know, but Chris said—"

"Hold on. Why would Chris text you and not me? You

know what? Now, that I'm thinking about it, yo' phone upstairs. How you know Chris at ProHealth in Waukesha?" He turned in his seat and faced me while we were at a stop light.

"I uhmm—"

"Gi' my phone." He gently snatched his phone from my hand. "Oh, you was reading these texts from Kim, huh."

"It kept going off, I thought it was important. Ain't like I went looking for it. I just wanted to fry my man some wings." I turned and looked out the window as he glanced over her messages.

"You coulda blocked this shit," he mumbled more to himself than me. "Damn, I ain't know Steven was her pops. Wait—oh, that's nasty."

"What's nasty?"

"I'll tell you later. You gonna be OK?" he questioned once we got to the hospital, parking his truck in the garage across the street.

"Yeah. Where you going?"

"Upstairs to see what's going on with my brother."

"I'm going too! You not 'bout to leave me. There go X right there." I pointed at Deo's number-one street general moving quickly between the rows. "Where's Chris?"

"Stay right here." Deo jumped out of the truck before I could get another word out.

By this time, Xander was jogging back to his car. He turned around too late as Deo's pistol connected with his skull, knocking him out cold. Leaving him on the pave-

ment as he walked swiftly back to the truck, Deo ignored
me, instead popping the lift gate and digging around for a
second before he found what he was looking for. I watched
as he then went back and duct taped X's mouth, tying him
up with the precision of a Boy's Scout before patting down
his pockets. Holding something small in the air, he pointed
it at the back of the lot before grabbing X by the ankles
and pulling him two rows over. I picked up his phone to
call Chris to come and help, but from the looks of it, Deo
was good. Thank God no one was in the garage watching
as the trunk door on a black car opened out of nowhere,
and Deo tossed him in. I didn't know my man had *that*
much strength. Maybe I need to shut my mouth half the
time.

"Did you call Chris?" he questioned as if he hadn't just
stuffed a six-foot grown man in the trunk of a car.

"Uhmm... no, not yet."

"Gimme the phone, Jordynn." Deo slid his iPhone from
my frozen fingers. I was still in shock from what I just saw.
"Lil' bro, what's good?"

"Shit." Chris sighed in the phone's speaker. "Just had to
chump ya mans off up here at this hospital, but I'm
straight."

"What happened?" I called out so he knew I was in
the car.

"Hey, sis. So Deo, check it, I call this nigga up here
because Doc admitted Tandra for monitoring—"

"What! She not due yet!" I rubbed our baby bump worriedly.

"Right, sis. I said the same thing. We came up here 'cause she cramping, said something didn't feel right. They put him on the lil' machine, and *blam*! He got an arrythmia."

"Where did he get that from?" Deo stroked his beard, staring absently out the front window.

"Nobody knows. You know Doc say, 'oh, sometimes these things happen and correct themselves.'"

"Yeah, they gotta tell you that so they don't get sued." Deo spoke thoughtfully.

"Right. So I text the nigga X, tell him to slide through so we can chat. Even if it wasn't about the baby being mine, I just wanted him to know where his girl at, right?"

"Right." Deo and I spoke in unison.

"Soon as I text this clown, he walk in the room like he been there the whole time! So I'm looking at him crazy. Meanwhile, Tandra turned white as snow. So now I'm like, 'OK, this nigga got her scared.' NOW I'M INTRIGUED. So I start talking, and this nigga put his hand up and fucking shushes me like I'm some lil' ass kid!"

"Whaaaat!" Deo sat up in his seat. I could tell from the look on his face he wasn't feeling Xander shushing his little brother.

"RIGHT! THAT'S WHAT I SAID! So I tell this nigga we need to talk, and he turn to Tandra and say, 'I know you ain't been out here hoeing around with these Stavros niggas.' I'm like, 'OK, nigga, them fighting words!' Nurse bust in the room and put both us out, telling us to get out the hospital before she have us arrested... yadda, yadda, yadda."

"So what X doing while she talking?" Deo wanted to know.

"X staring at me like he wanna do something, so you know me, I'm like, 'what's up?' Nurse tell us we can't be scrapping in the hospital, a baby's LIFE is at stake. You know I'm already on go mode; I'm 'bout to go back in the room, and this nigga X SWINGS ON ME!"

"He what?"

"YES, DEO! YA BOY SWUNG ON ME! So I duck, he end up putting his fist through the wall, and I pieced him up real quick before security escorted his dumb ass out tha hospital."

"So you straight?"

"I'm good. Can't believe he said that to her though. I'm 'bout to go in here now and get some information from her. She gotta tell me something; X ain't the nigga she need to be scared of when she carrying my son."

"Facts. Aye, me and wife down here in the parking lot. You want her to come up?"

"Oh, yeah, yeah, yeah. She can slide through. That way, Tandra not up here by herself. I gotta go find this nigga X."

"I know where he at. Come downstairs, and we can go handle this now."

"A'ight, bet. Sis, Tandra in room 512."

"OK, Chris, here I come." Deo hit the button to disconnect the call, chuckling at the story he just heard. "Be good, Deo."

"Baby, I'm always good. Whatchu talking about?"

"I'm not playing with you, Deo. Be good."

"Alright, I will." He leaned over and gave me a peck on the cheek before sliding his tongue between my lips. "Why you taste like pineapples?"

"Because I got a husband." I smiled back. "Wives supposed to taste tropical."

"I'll keep that in mind next time I—"

"Bye, Deo." I mushed his head playfully before I got out of our truck. I had to admit, seeing Deo knock Xander out and toss him in that trunk had me wet. I loved it when he smelled all masculine and shit. I was so focused on his scent that I didn't see the red Buick speeding toward me as I crossed the street until it was too late...

27

Kim

When Deo called and said we needed to talk, I was positive he was gonna ask me to move back in. With everything going wrong in my life, knowing he was still thinking about me, let me know I had his heart. He was only with Jordynn out of guilt for being the reason I killed her twin. If he really was upset, I would be in jail or worse.

My mother was serious this time when she told me to get out. I came back to my clothes thrown across her front yard ripped into shreds. I called the police on her, enough was enough. I didn't have the money to buy all new things. If anything, now I had to put a roof over my head. The police escorted me inside the house where I found out that she stole the money I put up for me to move. All $7,000 of my money was gone. Then this bitch had the nerve to tell the police I was lying, and I ain't have no money because I didn't have a job. Since I couldn't prove it, I had to take the L.

I'd been going back and forth staying in shelters, but lately, each one I went to claimed they didn't have room. I'd been sleeping in the back seat of my car for about a week now, and with this baby growing bigger by the day, I needed room to move around. I needed some help, and not from either off my parents. Off the top of my head, the only other person I could think of besides Steven that would cash me out was Ronnie. I hadn't seen him in a while, and I knew his mother would be too happy seeing my baby bump. I called him up and he answered on the second ring:

"Hey, babe!" Silence. "Ronnie?"

"Mmm... ssss... right there, baby," a woman's voice cooed in the background. "That feel so good. I know she can't do this, can she?"

"Oh—ooohhh, naw. She don't do that," Ronnie's voice replied. "I told you we ain't engaged for real. That shit was for my mama."

"Well, now that yo' mama know you like dick, SHE CAN GO NOW!" The voice's cadence changed from a high alto to a deep bass. "Yeah, that's right, bitch! I know you on the phone! You blocked now! BLING! BOOM! BUH-BYE BITCH!"

My phone dropped to the floor of my car as the tears began to well up in my eyes. First Deo, then my own mother, my father basically told me he wanted to keep fucking me knowing I was his daughter, and now trade had his bitch dump me over the phone. We not gonna even mention the fact that Zane stopped answering his phone for me. At the very least, I thought we were friends. These past few weeks had been rough. Even as an only child I'd never felt so alone in my life.

"Wait... David! I wonder if he's still in the States," I mumbled, fumbling for my phone. Finding his number, I hit talk, praying he was here and in a good mood. I sent up a small prayer to whoever listened when he answered.

"Hey... Kim?"

"Hi, David. How are you?"

"Uhmm... a little shocked right now, but that's neither here nor there."

"Shocked? What happened?'

"Just found out I have a son."

I rubbed my baby bump worriedly. David was also a potential father for this child. As much as I hoped it was Deo's, I ultimately had to face the reality of my situation. "Oh, wow! How is the mother doing?"

"She died twenty years ago." David's voice sounded far away, further than our little corner of Wisconsin.

"How is that possible?"

David seemed to snap out of his daze. I wondered what that was all about. "Never mind. So what's going on with you?"

"Funny you mention you have a son." I continued to

drag my hand in semicircles around my belly. "We really need to talk."

"Sure. When would you like to chat?"

"Tonight?" If I could get some money out of him today, I wouldn't have to sleep in my car again tonight.

"Ehhh... tonight might not be a good idea."

"Oh, are you out of the country?"

"No, no, I'm in Wisconsin. I'm gonna try and get in contact with my son while I'm here. Maybe we'll go out for dinner or something. I don't know."

"Want me to come too? I can be your moral support, just in case. Plus, I'd love to meet your son."

"Oh, no, that won't be necessary. I don't want Jordynn to be uncomfortable. I never implied I was in a relationship with anyone when we met."

"Jordynn?"

"Yes, Jordynn. My son's wife."

"Your—your son wouldn't be Deo Stavros, is he?"

"Yes, you know him?"

Oh my God... not again... "David, I gotta let you go. Give me a call later, OK?"

"Take care, Kim." He hurried off the phone, not even acknowledging that we needed to talk later.

Throwing my phone against the passenger side door, I screamed until my throat was sore. Wetness spilled from my orbs freely and cascaded down my cheeks. What had I done in a former life that would make God treat me like this? All the men in this damn city... what were the odds that I'd have sex not just with my own brother, but my father, my boyfriend, his brother, *and* his father too? And if it wasn't bad enough that my pussy had a high body count, I was pregnant. True enough, this baby wasn't Maurice's, but for what it was worth, I would've been better off if he was in the running too. At least he would've made sure I was good, unlike the rest of these selfish bastards.

With my current situation being what it was, I almost called my mother back and apologized, but in hindsight, I wouldn't give that bitch the satisfaction. She thought she broke me, but this time, I wasn't running back home to hide under her titty. *Oh, you hate me, huh? Well, I'm gonna have the last laugh this time, you toxic bitch.*

Out of nowhere, a sharp pain shot through my side, doubling me over in agony. I reached out to start my car, but a second throbbing wave crippled me from the waist down. I looked around for my phone to call for help, noticing that it fell between the seat. The pain subsided just enough for me to feel the smooth screen with my fingertips before antagonizing me a third time. I rolled my window down to scream for help when I felt a wet stickiness between my thighs. "Help me..." I whispered raggedly to the universe before my lower body went into spasms again. Closing my eyes, I wept as time stood still. For reasons that would forever be unknown to me, my body was beginning to reject the life growing inside me.

The street I was parked on was quiet... too quiet. Quiet enough for no one to hear my pleas for assistance, quiet enough for my baby to begin his premature escape from my womb, quiet enough for me to realize that my child was slipping away from me, and there was no way for me to stop it. Never could I hear his or her little cries. Never would I hold him in my arms. Never would I have someone who loved me unconditionally for me being me. Never would I know the feeling of pure love, *real* love from a small human who looked at me with nothing but true love, not the superficial love that I was able to make random men feel with my body. *Oh, God, please... please send someone to help me...*

When I opened my eyes I noticed the cramping subsided, but I still felt a small puddle between my legs. Instinctively, I knew I had to go to the hospital. With no prenatal care and knowing I was still drinking in the clubs every night, I knew there was nothing that could be done to save the baby at this point. I'd had a D&C done before when I had some abnormal bleeding, but this time the surgical procedure would be to remove the remnants of my child. That's all my baby was reduced to at this point— remnants. Remnants of what might have been. Remnants of a life lost. Remnants of a future that now would never be. Remnants...

The sun was setting by the time I pulled up to ProHealth Memorial in Waukesha and I was tired, both physically and mentally. With everything that transpired in the past couple of hours, I still had to get out of this car and make my way to the emergency room alone. As I drove toward the circular driveway to park hopefully a little closer, I thought my eyes were deceiving me when I saw... *her.*

Jordynn.

The bitch that stole my man and my life.

Oh she's happy, huh?

She's *happy.*

Everything became a blur as I focused in on her round baby bump that she had the nerve to reach out and rub as she took her time crossing the street. She knew I was coming to this hospital. She knew what she was doing.

Taunting me.

Mocking me.

Why else would she be here?

What about me, bitch. What about my baby!

Her body hit the front of my car first, flipping across the hood and landing on my windshield as her surprised glare haunted me through the glass. Blood covered her face, her eyes agape and focused on nothing for a second longer before slowly closing shut. She didn't even see me coming.

Bitches bleed just like us, Jordynn. I'll kill a pregnant hoe too.

To Be Continued...

I'M GONNA BE HONEST, even I wasn't expecting that ending! Kim has definitely crossed the line, and I'm here for part 3! Are you? Subscribe to my mailing list at www. fatimasbooks.com for updates and sneak peeks!

Get caught up on Part 1: http://bit.ly/PGLS33
Join my reading group on Facebook! http://facebook.com/ groups/ReadingWithFatima
Do you have IG? Follow me! http:// instagram.com/fatima_munroe
Are you on Twitter? Follow me! http:// twitter.com/fatima_munroe

Thanks for rocking with me! Don't forget to drop that review!

Coming 05/16!

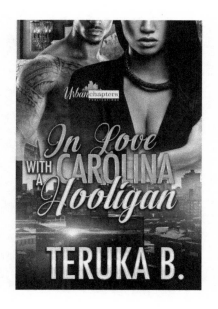

CPSIA information can be obtained
at www.ICGtesting.com
Printed in the USA
LVHW091750270619
622553LV00005B/862/P